Caught in the Current

PACIFIC SHORES
- BOOK 2 -

Caught in the Current

PACIFIC SHORES
- BOOK 2 -

Brynn Stewart

PACIFIC SHORES SERIES

Contemporary Christian Romance

Beyond the Waves – BOOK ONE

Caught in the Current – BOOK TWO

Song of the Surf – BOOK THREE

Written in the Sand – BOOK FOUR

Other books by Brynn Stewart

THE RIVERSONG SERIES

Contemporary Christian Romance

Angel Kisses and Riversong – BOOK ONE

Soft Kisses and Birdsong – BOOK TWO

Butterfly Kisses and Windsong – BOOK THREE

HEARTS OF HOLLYWOOD

Contemporary Christian Romance Novellas

My Blue Havyn – BOOK ONE

Mistletoe and Mochas – BOOK TWO

Kittens and Snow Flurries – BOOK THREE

MISTY COVE

Contemporary Christian Romance Novellas

The Heart of Christmas – BOOK ONE

The Wonder of Christmas – BOOK TWO

Caught in the Current
PACIFIC SHORES, Book 2

Cover design by Lynnette Bonner of Indie Cover Design
images ©
www.depositphotos.com, File: # 87815092 - couple
www.adobestock.com, File: #178916592 - beach

Author photo © Emily Hinderman, EMH Photography

ISBN: 978-1-942982-55-5

Printed in the U.S.A.

2 Corinthians 5:17–19

Therefore, if anyone is in Christ, the new
creation has come: The old has gone,
the new is here!
All this is from God, who
reconciled us to himself through Christ
and gave us the ministry of reconciliation: that God
was reconciling the world to himself in Christ, not
counting people's sins against them.
And he has committed to us the message of
reconciliation.

Chapter 1

"Alyssa Anne Sinclair, you come back here right now!" Marie dashed down the cereal aisle after her precocious three-and-a-half-year-old.

"But Mommy, I want the chocate kind. Wif mashmallows." Alyssa stopped directly in front of a box at kid eye level with enough cartoon characters on it to start a new animation network.

Marie sighed and squatted down next to her daughter. Running one hand over her little one's disarrayed hair, she pondered several things all at once. First, how did Alyssa's hair always end up in so many tangles only an hour into the day? Second, how was she going to talk her out of the chocolate cereal that should come standard with a vial of insulin? And third, and certainly not least, what was she going to do if she couldn't find a sitter?

She certainly couldn't afford to take time off work. And Taysia was already much too kind to her when it came to taking time away from the gym to be with Alyssa. The problem was, she'd known for several months that Mrs. Hernandez was moving to Arizona to live near her daughter. Just...procrastination had gotten the better of her—again. Now she had a week to figure this out, or she'd be forced to request time off.

Beside her, Alyssa pooched out her lower lip and gave her a good dose of the best pleading expression she could apparently muster. Marie bit back a grin. She had to have a heart of stone, because the look wasn't doing much for her.

"Honey, I know Aunt Taysia and Uncle Kylen let you have that kind sometimes when you go to their house, but it's really not good for you. Mom grabbed you the crunchy kind with raspberries that you like so much." She resisted the urge to stick her tongue into her cheek and prayed Alyssa would fall for it.

"But I only like that kind when the chocate kind isn't in the cupboard."

"Well." Marie stood and tried another tactic. "I'm sorry, but I don't have enough money to buy both, so we have to leave this one here today." She cringed, knowing how ineffective that argument would be, since her three-year-old had no understanding of income versus expense.

"But Mommy!" Big tears pooled on Alyssa's lower lids.

Oh boy, here we go. "Hey, how about if we go pick out some yogurt for you to pack in your lunches this week, Superwoman?"

"Yogurt! Yum!" With one blink, and not even a telephone booth in sight, the transformation from pout to glee was complete, and Alyssa dashed down the aisle.

Swinging the cart around, Marie called, "Wait for me, sweetheart. And no running in the store, please."

Alyssa obediently slowed to the fastest "walk" she could possibly muster.

Yogurt. Who knew? Marie tucked that little weapon into her mommy arsenal for future reference.

Alyssa disappeared around the end of the aisle, and Marie picked up the pace, even though she wasn't really worried. Marinville was a fairly small, quiet town, and almost everyone knew and loved Alyssa, who'd never known a stranger.

But before her cart had even reached the main section by the yogurts, there came the loud crash of breaking glass, a masculine grunt, and a three-year-old gasp.

Marie cringed to a halt and held her breath, sure more damage loomed. She could envision a whole endcap display crashing to the ground.

Thankfully, only Alyssa's voice broke the silence. "Uh-oh! Sorry!"

Alyssa did sound truly sorry, but her repentance didn't ease the stone of dread that dropped into Marie's stomach. Whatever had just broken sounded expensive, and she was going to have to pay for it. Why hadn't she insisted Alyssa sit in the cart, like a normal mother would have?

Well, the only thing to do was to go see what had happened. She started forward.

"Hey there, Superwoman. I'm sorry—I should have been watching where I was going more carefully, I guess."

Marie jerked the cart to a stop with such force her stack of soup cans toppled.

That voice. He really was here! Her heart lodged in her throat, and she prayed Alyssa would come looking for her so she could go down the aisle the other way and not have to face the man currently talking to her daughter. She'd known he was supposed to be coming home to help his mother run their bed-and-breakfast, since his dad's cancer had taken his strength.

Still...maybe it wasn't really him? She froze and listened with all her might.

"Hey!" Alyssa's tone rang with indignation. "How did you know I am Superwoman?"

Marie heard the sound of glass tinking together and some scuffling like he was using his foot to scoot the shattered shards into a pile. "Well, by the big *S* on your pink shirt, I guess."

"You're tall."

The man chuckled.

A sweet sensation like a drizzle of honey on sourdough toast settled into the pit of Marie's stomach. How long had it been since she'd heard that oh-so-familiar, gentle laugh? *Reece Cahill.* Marie's eyes dropped closed. It really was him.

"I guess I am tall, now that you mention it." A boot squeaked on the tiles, and this time when Reece spoke, his voice seemed to be coming to her from a drastically de-elevated level. "How's that? Better?"

"You have eyes like grass. My mommy likes grass eyes."

Reece's chuckle again, full of curiosity this time. "Grass eyes?"

"You know, the color of grass."

"Oh!" Reece's boots squeaked on the tiles again. "Speaking of your mommy"—his voice emerged slightly muffled—"is she around here someplace, tyke? Do you know her name?"

Marie jolted into action. Great. Now he would think she was a terrible mother who couldn't even keep track of one little girl, on top of all the other things he already knew about her. She forced one foot in front of the other and rolled her cart out into the open.

Reece squatted on the balls of his feet before Alyssa.

His typical attire of cowboy boots, jeans, T-shirt, and Stetson hadn't changed over the years, she noted. What had changed was his lankiness. The man was no longer tall and straight. He was tall and...chiseled. There was no other way to put it. He'd always been strong and athletic, but now...muscles stretched his T-shirt in all the right places to mouthwatering degrees.

She swallowed and focused on her daughter, who stood right in front of the man with his cheeks cupped in her chubby hands as she closely—very closely—examined his eyes. Eyes Marie well remembered, and likely the reason green was her favorite color.

Reece must have caught sight of her shoes, because he tipped his head ever so slightly and peered around her daughter. His gaze started at her grimy, Saturday-chore tennis shoes and traveled all the way up past her jogging shorts and paint-splattered T-shirt to her face.

His eyes rounded. "Marie!" He stood slowly, reflexively picking up Alyssa and settling her on one very sinewy forearm. He pushed his hat back on his head and swept a glance from her head to ankles and back again. Then he looked from her to Alyssa, a light of understanding dawning on his face. His focus dropped to where Marie's ringless left hand rested on the handle of the shopping cart.

Marie's face flamed so hot it likely could have sizzled bacon. Yeah, he probably wouldn't be surprised to note she still wasn't married. "Hi, Reece. I'm really sorry about all this." She swiped a gesture to the three jars of pickles broken open by his feet. "Just tear off the bar codes, and I'll pay for them when I get to the front."

Oh boy... She resisted the urge to cringe, and really hoped that hadn't sounded like she'd done this before half a dozen times...or so. She chanced a glance at his face.

But Reece's attention had zoned in on her daughter, his head pulled back to make focusing on Alyssa's face easier. "You're an old pro at this, huh?"

Alyssa shrugged. "Mommy says my feet move faster than my brain sometimes."

To his credit, Reece withheld the bark of laughter Marie could tell wanted to burst forth. He only nodded sagely. "You know, I think my feet did a lot of going faster than my brain when I was your age too."

"Really?" Alyssa swung a look her way. "Mommy, he broke pickles too!"

Marie smiled, but all she really wanted to do was escape from the presence of the only man she'd ever had any real feelings for. From the only man who'd ever broken her heart. She stretched a hand out to her daughter. "Come on, Superwoman, we need to go find someone to clean this up. Then we need to grab your yogurt and get back home."

Reece complied with her unspoken request and put Alyssa on the floor. Marie took her little convict's hand in a firm grip.

"Welcome home. Nice to see you again," she offered in parting and hurried to make her getaway.

But as she started away, Alyssa stiffened and hung back. "Mommy, we have to get the scanny things so we can pay."

"Right."

Drat. No chance for escape yet.

"And I don't want to do dishes this time. That was no fun."

Marie pressed her lips together and didn't meet Reece's gaze. He had remained stock still, his hands resting on slim hips. He probably thought she and

Alyssa had come here straight from the loony bin. "Well...you have to do something to work off your debt. We've talked about running in the store lots of times. This"—she held a hand out to the spreading puddle of pickle juice—"is what happens when you do." She was trying to tamp down her irritation and keep her words loving, but as if it wasn't bad enough that Alyssa had done something like this again, it had to have been Reece!

She squatted next to the mess of pickles and glass.

Where had he been for all these years, anyway? She hadn't seen him since...when? Four years at least. She'd still been pregnant with Alyssa when she'd heard he'd left town, and no one seemed to know where he'd gone off to.

As she found the shards of the jars with the bar codes and worked to pull one of them free, she noticed he'd been buying some sort of organic, all-natural pickles. Of course he had. Because Alyssa couldn't have run into someone buying just one jar of the el cheapo store brand. Why was he buying three jars of pickles, anyhow? This was probably going to cost her at least fifteen bucks after tax. She mentally recalculated the items already in her cart that she could return to the shelf.

Reece was suddenly squatting by her side. "Listen, this really wasn't all her fault. I was carrying three jars of these things, and if I hadn't left my cart over there by the cold foods section, the jars never would have fallen. Why don't you let me cover it just this once?"

Simply his nearness and the sound of his voice were doing things to her pulse that could set off all sorts of alarms if she were hooked up to a monitor. She kept her focus on the floor, not daring to meet his eyes. "No. No. I couldn't let you pay. If she hadn't been running, your pickles would have made it to your cart just fine."

Why was this sticker being so stubborn about coming off the glass? The thing was soaked in pickle juice; if anything, the liquid should help it come loose easier.

"Your daughter is beautiful." His words were low and raspy.

That did it. She stood and tucked a strand of hair behind her ear. "Thank you. Nice seeing you again. Alyssa, come on, honey." She would just take the whole broken piece to the register and tell them to ring up three of them.

Reece rose with her. "Marie..." His tone said she was being stubborn.

Well, that may be, but she wasn't about to let him pay for Alyssa's rambunctiousness. She chose to ignore his chiding. And the fact that he hadn't taken his gaze off her face for the past several minutes.

Alyssa had ignored her call and squatted next to a seep of pickle juice. Chubby hands resting against little knees, she scooted along with it, following the trickling green river as it expanded across the tiles.

As Marie reached to set the broken jar into the child seat on the cart, her peripheral vision caught one chubby hand reaching toward a shard of glass. "Alyssa! Don't touch that! I don't want you getting cut." She glanced over to ensure her daughter was going to listen, but doing so made her hand miss the seat. Her grip slipped on the juice-greased glass. With a jolt she tried to catch it. A sharp slice of pain angled across the pad of her finger and over one knuckle. She hissed and reflexively dropped the piece of the jar, which shattered it into several more shards.

Reece was immediately by her side.

She had instinctively clamped the fingers of her other hand around the injury.

He reached for it. "Let me see." He stepped so close his hat brim brushed her cheek when he leaned forward to look at the cut. His touch was gentle and probably meant to be soothing.

But her heart had apparently received some sort of errant signal, because it was beating fast enough to count as aerobic exercise.

A low sound of distress rumbled in his throat. "This is pretty deep. I think you are going to need stitches."

Sure, that was just what she needed. A doctor bill.

She snatched her hand from his grasp. "I'll be fine, I'm sure. Nothing a Band-Aid won't fix."

She examined her finger. A flap of skin gaped open, and blood was already dripping on the floor. The glass had somehow managed to slice down the side of her finger also. Oh boy. That cut was a doozy. Old, familiar words that used to be part of her everyday vocabulary sprang to mind, and she clamped her teeth shut before any of them could pop out. But she had to do something. "Ah. Okay." She couldn't seem to think. *Do not panic. Do not panic.*

She'd never been too good around the sight of blood, though she'd gotten a little better at handling it now that she was a single mother of an accident-prone toddler.

They really could not go to the hospital. Her insurance only covered 70 percent of emergency room visits, and she couldn't even afford an extra dollar in her budget right now, much less who knew how much.

Plus she had things she needed to get done. Tomorrow was her day to bring the weekly treat for their

Sunday school class, so she needed to get her cinnamon rolls baked. And she had a second coat of paint to put on the last wall of the unit next door for Mr. Meyer, her apartment complex manager, before she earned the extra hundred bucks she needed to pay all her bills this month.

She needed...Band-Aids. She glanced at the injury again. Okay, butterfly Band-Aids. A wave of light-headedness drained through her.

Marie turned a sickly pale greenish color. "Whoa." Reece's stomach clenched, and he lurched toward her and gripped both of her shoulders. He bent down and peered into her face. "Take a breath, Marie." He smoothed his hands from her shoulders to her elbows and back again.

Even though she complied, she still didn't look quite right, and she was trembling.

"Good. And another." Heaven help him, even in paint-splattered work clothes, she was more beautiful than he'd remembered. She had eyes so blue a man felt like he could dive right into the cool depths of them. But right now they were wide and terrified as she studied the cut on her finger.

He let go of her shoulders and took hold of her cut hand, clamping his own fist around the now severely bleeding digit. "Alyssa." He snapped his fingers at the little girl, who was apparently engrossed in the moving green liquid. "How would you like to take a ride with me and your mom in my big blue truck?"

Alyssa leapt to her feet. "Yes!"

Good. Looked like he'd pegged her right. Always up for a new adventure, just like her mother was. His gaze skittered back to Marie. *Or at least used to be.*

She still looked like she was about to hurl. Maybe she didn't like doctors? "A few stitches and you'll be as good as new."

"Reece, I really can't—"

But just then the box boy stepped into view. "Excuse me?" Reece cut her off.

The kid, who had to be about sixteen, stepped over, his eyes widening as he took in the chaos surrounding them.

Reece gestured from the drips of blood around their feet to the splat of pickles and glass in the aisle. "Could you clean this up for us, please? And put that grocery cart there"—he pointed to his groceries down by the cold stuffs—"and this cart here"—he pointed to hers—"off to the side somewhere? I'll be back to get it all in about an hour."

The kid scratched his head and examined the mess, his eyes darting from the pickles to the blood and back again, as though wondering which disaster to clean up first.

Marie cringed. "I'm really sorry, Alex."

Reece's eyebrows went up. She obviously knew the kid. How many times had the poor guy had to clean up after them? He fleetingly wondered how many other mothers in the world were on a first-name basis with the cleanup crew at their grocery stores.

But Alex didn't seem fazed. "Oh, don't worry, Miss Sinclair. We employees sort of had a bet—" His eyes shot wide and he spun on one heel, making a hasty retreat as he called over one shoulder, "Don't worry, I'll clean it up, and yeah, I'll have the carts waiting for you, sir."

Reece grinned down at her. "I think Alyssa might have just made that boy some money."

"How nice that my daughter's accident proneness can be fodder for an excellent gaming economy at Thrift and Save." Marie's face turned the prettiest shade of pink he'd seen in a long time. Her hand felt fragile under his. She was still as small and delicate as he remembered.

He swallowed. Four years of running from his feelings for her, and his first full day back in town, he met her at the grocery store. What were the odds? She wasn't wearing a ring—he gave himself a mental shake. A woman like her would certainly have a man in her life. And it was best he remember that—*and* the reason he'd broken things off with her in the first place. There was no evidence anything had changed.

Get back to the business at hand. He almost rolled his eyes at the inadvertent pun. "We should go."

"Listen. I don't need a doctor. Just a Band-Aid." She looked a trifle terrified at the thought of going to the hospital.

Reece's eyes narrowed. He didn't want to scare her further, but he'd definitely seen the white of bone where the cut had crossed over her knuckle.

Her chin lifted in an oh-so-familiar stubborn tilt.

Then again, maybe giving her a good dose of reality was the only way to get her to do what was needed. He shook his head. "Band-Aid's not going to be enough. You need a doctor. The cut is really deep. And do you know how many germs could be on the glass? It was on the floor before it cut you. Besides, the way the cut looked, you could have sliced a tendon. You need to have it looked at."

Marie ran her free hand back through her hair. Her finger, still firmly in Reece's grasp, was throbbing to beat the band, and despite his death hold on it, blood still seemed to be leaking out. She probably did need a doctor. She dropped her free hand to her side in frustration. She would just have to try and find a couple more odd jobs this month. “Fine.”

“That’s my girl.”

Marie darted him a look as her heart did a double flip. Of course he hadn’t meant the words to be anything more than encouragement. But the feel of his warm fingers around hers was much too enjoyable even if he was only trying to keep her from bleeding to death. She didn’t want her heart falling into that undertow again. It was nothing but a riptide that could tear her apart.

“Here, just...” She grabbed up the hem of her T-shirt and indicated he should let go of her finger. The second he let go, blood seeped into the space and started to drip on the floor again. She clamped a wad of her T-shirt around it. She offered him a flick of a glance. “We better take my car. I don’t want to get blood all over your truck.”

Reece pushed out his lower lip, wiped his bloody palm on his jeans, and snagged a set of keys from his front pocket. “No worries.”

She darted a glance at her purse where it sat in her cart. “Could you...” Before she could figure out exactly what she wanted him to do with it, he’d picked it up and looped the strap around her neck, angling it across her body so it settled against one hip.

“Good?” He was so close she could see the flecks of amber in his irises.

Mouth dry, she nodded.

“Let’s just take my truck. It will be easier for me to drive you. Besides, I already promised Alyssa here a ride, didn’t I, kid? You ready to go?” He squatted down to floor level. “Hop onto my back, and we’ll take your mom to get her finger looked at."

"I love piggyback rides!" Alyssa gave a little squeal and clambered aboard.

Leaping to his feet, Reece gave a distinct whinny. He snagged his Stetson from his head and plopped it back onto Alyssa's curls, then leapt a couple of trots ahead. "No pigs around here. Only horses."

Marie shook her head and followed them down the aisle at a much more sedate pace.

Alyssa giggled and used one hand to push back the much-too-large hat. "You're funny. Do you want to be my daddy?"

Marie gasped and tripped over her own feet.

Chapter 2

Thankfully Marie caught herself before she sprawled flat right there in the main aisle. But if ever she'd wanted the floor to open up and swallow her, this was it.

Reece only let out a bark of laughter and spun around to walk backward, assessing her with glimmering green eyes. "You don't have a daddy, huh?"

While he'd directed the question at her daughter, there was a simmering curiosity in his gaze that flooded Marie with heat.

"Nope. Mr. Jackson wants to be my daddy, and Mommy said maybe. But he's not—"

"—Alyssa!"

Blessedly, for once in her life, Alyssa seemed to catch on to the fact that Marie didn't want her to share further, and she let the rest of whatever she'd planned to say drop.

A breath of relief pushed past Marie's lips. But just to ensure something like this never happened again, she focused a mother eye on Alyssa. "That is not a question you are to ask a man again—ever—do you understand?"

"But Mommy, why? I think he would be a fun daddy, don't you?"

"No!"

Reece winced and jammed a fist over his heart as though holding onto the handle of a knife she'd just thrust there.

Marie resisted a smile at his theatrics. "Well...maybe."

Reece's eyebrows shot up.

She hurried on before he could comment. "But that's not how getting a daddy works."

Oh boy, this was a mess. Had she really just said maybe? And right after Alyssa had mentioned Dan? Reece was going to think she hadn't changed a smidge since he broke up with her in high school.

Reece seemed to be having just a bit too much fun with this. He tucked his lower lip between his teeth, squinched up his face, and tilted his head, as though seriously assessing her answer. Then she noted the glimmer of amusement crinkling the corners of his eyes.

The man was laughing at her predicament! She wrinkled her nose at him.

He grinned and, after a quick wink, faced forward again.

She couldn't deny her relief at being free from his scrutiny.

Alyssa had apparently been pondering her response, because just then she piped up with "How does getting a daddy work, then?"

Reece gave a distinct snort, but mercifully he didn't turn to look at her this time.

The automatic sliding doors opened for them, and they stepped out into the warm July heat of the Pacific coast. Maybe she could just change the subject. "We'll need to get Alyssa's car seat from my car."

Reece seemed to take pity on her and joined in the effort. "Sure. Where are you parked?"

She gestured as best she could with her T-shirt-compressed finger toward her ancient, rust-marbled white Toyota Corolla. And of course the keys were in her purse. She fumbled with trying to keep the compression on her finger and lift the flap on her purse at the same time.

"Here, let me." Reece stepped close, but then paused. "Do you mind?"

It wasn't like she was going to have an easy time getting the keys out herself. She might as well complete her lesson in humiliation and get it over with. She shook her head. "Go ahead. Thanks."

As Reece set to digging through her purse, she considered their driving situation again. "We really should just take my car. We'll have to come right back by here on our way home from the hospital, and I can just drop you off at your truck, and then we won't have to transfer the car seat back and forth."

"But Mommy! I want to ride in the big blue truck!"

Reece scrunched one eye closed and offered her an apologetic look, even as he lifted her keys on one finger. "Tell you what, kiddo." He swung Alyssa down to the pavement and bent to look into her face.

Marie loved the way he got right down to Alyssa's level when he communicated with her. Something went soft inside her.

"How about we go get your mom's finger fixed up at the hospital, then we come back here to get groceries, and then you and your mom can ride in my truck to the welcome-home barbeque my parents are hosting for me tonight?" He angled a questioning look at her over his shoulder.

"Yes! Yes! Yes!" Alyssa was already clapping her hands and jumping up and down.

All the softness Marie had just been feeling hardened into granite. How could she say no when he'd just gotten Alyssa's hopes so high? But she really must say no. She still had so much to get done. "No, I'm sorry. We can't." Of course she couldn't say the real reason they couldn't go—the fact that Reece's mother had handed out invitations to everyone around her at church on Sunday but not given her one—because to do so would just sound like a cry for pity. "Can we just..." She let the words trail away and blinked hard at the asphalt under her feet. All she really wanted to do was go back home and crawl into bed and sleep for several hours. But that was not going to happen.

Exhaustion pressed down on her. She'd already worked five eight-hour shifts at the gym this week, plus put in several hours after Alyssa was asleep each night painting the apartment across the hall for her landlord just to get a hundred bucks.

If Reece wasn't careful, he was going to end up with one very emotional female to deal with.

"Please, Mommy? Please? Please? Please?!"

Great, now the tears were going to start in earnest. She really could use some emotionally stress-free days. Were two in a row too much to ask for? She gritted her teeth against the flood of emotion wanting to burst forth and didn't even bother answering Alyssa for the moment.

Reece took one look at her face and lurched into motion. "Hey, kiddo, I'll tell you what. If it doesn't work out today, I'll give you a ride one of these days when I can figure out a good time with your mom, okay? Right now let's just get your mom fixed up." He unlocked the door and held it until Alyssa could climb inside. "Do you need help buckling your seatbelt?" he questioned her daughter.

Alyssa's lip was extended in a full pout. "No. I can do it myself."

"Gotcha." Reece shut the door and turned to face Marie. "I'm really sorry. I wasn't thinking what a spot that would put you in. I'll be more careful in the future."

In the future? Marie swallowed. She tipped him a nod of forgiveness.

He opened her door, and she sank into her seat while he trotted around to the driver's side. To her chagrin, she found that while her three-year-old hadn't needed help with her seat belt, she did. There was no way to keep the compression on her finger and pull the belt across her at the same time. In frustration she gave up. She could just ride to the hospital without one on.

But before she knew what he planned, Reece propped one arm behind her seat and leaned across her to grab her seat belt. For one split moment he paused and met her gaze, his face, shaded by the brim of his hat, only inches from hers. She smelled the crisp familiar scent of his aftershave and saw the glint of something inviting in his eyes. And then he eased back and clicked her belt in. He adjusted the driver's seat to give more room for his legs and turned the key.

Her car coughed a couple times but didn't catch right away.

"It always does that. You have to pump the gas a little." She tipped her head against the seat rest.

Reece pushed twice on the gas pedal and tried again.

Nothing.

Marie bit the inside of her lip. This was not happening to her, was it? She totally had no money to spend on her car. This day threatened to overwhelm her. She lolled her head over to look at the ocean across the road from Thrift and Save. It stretched into the distance, blue green meeting blue-gray sky on the sill of the horizon. She pressed her lips together and scrunched her eyes shut. She was not going to cry. Tears would not solve a single thing.

Reece engaged the starter several more times between pumps, all to no avail. He cleared his throat and glanced over at Marie.

Head back, she was staring out over the Pacific, and he could see the distinct shimmer of extra moisture in her eyes. He wanted to reach over and clasp her shoulder, but shoved his hands under his legs instead. He needed to remember why he'd walked away from her in the first place. He didn't know if she was any closer to the Lord now than she'd been, and no matter how beautiful she was, or how many emotions this woman could make him feel, one thing he did know was that he wanted a marriage where both he and his wife would put God first. Which clearly hadn't been the case with Marie the last time they'd been dating.

He shook off the memories. He really needed to get her in to have that finger fixed. "Let me grab my truck and give us a jump. Sit tight. Shouldn't take more than a minute."

He had to park behind her because there were no empty spaces nearby, but thankfully he had long enough cables. He parked, hooked up the cables, and tried the key again. Her little car still wouldn't start.

Marie looked weary.

He did squeeze her shoulder this time. *Only in a gesture of friendship.* "One thing at a time, huh? My truck to the hospital, and then I'll help you figure out what to do about your car."

She sighed softly. "Thanks."

"My pleasure." He clicked her seat belt open and then got out and unhooked the cables and jogged them back to his truck. By the time he returned to grab Alyssa, Marie had already wrestled open the back door. He rested a hand on her arm before she could try and lift Alyssa out. "I'll get her." The tyke was sound asleep, a little bunny he hadn't noticed before tucked under one arm.

Marie moved out of his way, smiling softly. "Can you lift both her and the seat at the same time? We can just leave her belted in and transfer her to your truck."

He grinned at the thought of her questioning whether he could lift a kid, who couldn't weigh twenty-five pounds soaking wet, and a car seat, which weighed maybe ten. The guys at Deschutes Rejuvenation would get a kick out of that. "Yeah, I think I can manage."

It didn't take him long to get both of them buckled into his truck.

As he put the truck in reverse, Marie spoke. "Thanks for driving me. I'm sorry we're going to end up taking up such a chunk of your day."

He shook his head and eased the truck out onto the main road. "It's not a problem, at all." A comfortable silence settled, but he really wanted to know a little more about her life. "So tell me about yourself."

His peripheral vision caught the lift of one slender shoulder. "Oh, you know. Pretty much the same as before, except I have a little girl now."

Disappointment settled.

"I still work at Mom's Gym with Taysia Sumner. Still live in the same apartment. What about you? Where have you been for the past several years?"

The hospital lay just ahead to the right. He put on

his blinker and pulled into the lot near the emergency room. "I've been working for a wilderness camp for troubled teen boys. They come to us from all sorts of backgrounds and live with us for six months. Hopefully they go home changed. I've loved it. But after eight rotations, I was feeling a little burnout. And then Dad took sick. So"—he shrugged—"I'm here to help Mom with the bed-and-breakfast for the foreseeable future."

"Oh."

Curiosity furrowed his brow as he stopped in a parking spot. Was it disappointment he heard in her tone? He glanced back at Alyssa. "Do you want me to take her out of her seat or just bring her seat in?"

Marie pressed her lips together. "If you don't mind holding her, I think she'll stay asleep longer than if we leave her in the seat."

"I don't mind at all." Carefully, he unbuckled the tyke and lifted her so her head lolled against his shoulder. Locking the truck, he shoved the keys into his pocket and then pressed a hand to Marie's back, directing her toward the emergency entrance.

Her feet seemed to drag until she finally came to a complete standstill. "Do you think I really need stitches?"

"Yes, I'm afraid you will. Listen, if it's the procedure that has you worried, I'll stay with you the whole time."

"No, it's not that. It's just—" She tucked one side of her lower lip between her teeth. "Never mind, let's just get this over with."

Chapter 3

Marie couldn't believe she'd almost blurted out that her finances were already stretched so thin she could read a book through them. Being around Reece was dangerous. He had a way of extracting things from her without her even knowing he was doing it.

The doors to the emergency room whooshed open, and the interior of the money-sucking facility loomed.

Okay, Lord, here we go. I could really use some help here. I'm sure You were looking over my shoulder when I was balancing my checkbook the other day? She paused. Why was it she never seemed to turn to God with her concerns before she worried and agonized about them till she was nearly a blubbering puddle? She winced a glance upward. *Forgive me? You are probably wishing I would learn to quit fretting about You providing so You could move on to some other lesson, huh? If I quit stressing, will You drop a big check from the sky?* She wrinkled her nose as they stopped before an unoccupied desk, behind which a door stood ajar. *Probably doesn't work like that, huh? I know. Okay, I'm trying to let this go. I trust You, I really do. And I'm so thankful for all the ways You've changed me. Help me to keep growing and learning to trust more.*

Reece wore a worried frown. "Are you okay?"

She nodded. "Yep. Just praying a little."

An emotion she couldn't quite peg softened his features and brightened his eyes. He opened his mouth like he wanted to respond, but just then a woman in blue scrubs bustled through the door and plopped into the chair behind the desk. She took in Reece and Alyssa first, and then her focus zoned in on Marie's bloody shirt. One eyebrow quirked. "What can we do for you today?"

Marie lifted the offending appendage still clamped carefully in her other fist. "I cut my finger."

The nurse was already pulling up a form on her computer. "I can see that. How did you cut it, and how deep did it look?"

"Uh...on a broken pickle jar, and I think it's pretty deep."

"How much pain are you in on a scale of one to ten? Ten being the most pain you've ever felt in your life."

Marie scrunched up her face. Did it matter if she wasn't in too much pain but might bleed a bucket on their floor? "Two, maybe three?"

The questions continued...and continued. Marie found a moment to be thankful Alyssa was sound asleep and that Reece was standing by so patiently and even digging out her insurance card for her when he really should be home with his groceries already. And then the dreaded words she'd known were coming.

"Your co-pay is seventy-five dollars. How would you like to pay for it today?"

Marie swallowed. It might as well be a thousand. She would just have to put it on the credit card she'd been trying to pay off. It still carried a good percentage of the medical costs she'd incurred when Alyssa was born a couple of weeks prematurely and had needed to stay extra days in the neonatal unit. And the percentage rate was outrageous, but she didn't have any other options.

She glanced apologetically at Reece. "Could you grab the Visa card in my wallet? It has an Oregon Duck logo on it."

Reece gave her an exaggerated wince as he angled his body so Alyssa would stay on his shoulder and dug into her purse for the third time that day. "The Ducks? Everyone knows OSU is the better school." He winked.

A tremor of awareness shot through her. She really needed to put the brakes on her disobedient emotions. She'd barely thought of Dan since she'd heard Reece's voice in the store, and then only because Alyssa had brought him up. Guilt niggled at her. After all, she'd promised the man she would think about his proposal.

Reece was eyeing her as though he expected a response.

She swallowed and shrugged. "The duck was cuter." And would have been the school of her choice if she hadn't gotten pregnant her senior year of high school.

Alyssa's sweet face came into focus. Even though she was the best mistake Marie had ever made, it still pained her to know she'd never be able to tell Alyssa the name of her father. Wasn't it going to be some conversation one day when Alyssa grew old enough to ask?

"Mom, who's my dad?"

"I don't know, honey, could be any one of a number of guys I met down at Pete's Bar."

Marie blinked herself back to the present and noticed Reece was still fumbling to find her card. It was only a moment before he seemed to recover, though, and he handed it to the nurse.

"All right, we'll just get you to sign the slip after we

can get your finger stitched up for you. Right this way, please."

Thirty minutes later, they were on their way out of the hospital parking lot, Marie with a numb finger that had required seven stitches and a prescription for antibiotics she probably shouldn't spend money on. Thankfully, they'd said she only nicked the tendon and it should heal up on its own.

It was only 1:00 p.m., but exhaustion gritted behind her eyelids, and there really wasn't anything at the grocery store they couldn't live without until tomorrow. Besides, if she didn't get away from this man's kind thoughtfulness real soon, she was going to forget she was as contented as a seagull at a picnic with her life just the way it was. Which was one of the reasons she'd been putting Dan off for a while now. "Reece, if you don't mind, could you just drop us at my apartment? I don't really need the groceries until tomorrow. I'll just go back and make another run at it after church."

He angled her a quick look, then returned his focus to the road. There was a bit of puzzlement on his face, but he only resettled his hat and said, "What about your prescription?"

She waved a hand and tried to come up with something that wouldn't be an outright lie. "Alyssa can finish her nap at home. And we live close to the pharmacy."

"Okay. Not a problem."

"Thanks. Just turn right on Coral. And I'm only a block down on the right."

"I remember. So...church? You still attend with Taysia?" Reece's thumbs tapped out a rhythm on the steering wheel.

"Oh, yeah, we all still go together."

"They picking you up?"

She frowned. "No. Why would they—Oh! My car!" She felt the burn of humiliation. He must think she was such a ditz. "Normally I drive Alyssa and me. But I'm sure they won't mind picking us up tomorrow. I'll just give them a call." What was she going to do about the betrayal of her Corolla? She pushed the thought aside. Her Judas of a car was a problem for another day.

He cleared his throat and turned on his blinker as Coral approached. "I can pick you up, if you like."

Hadn't she just been telling herself she needed to eschew the man's kindness? Yet, it would be easier just to have him get them. And she couldn't just skip tomorrow, because she was on for Sweet Inspirations. Maybe she should call Dan and have him get them? But he lived on the other side of the church from them.

She bit her lip in indecision for a moment before finally saying, "I guess if you don't mind, it would be a big help. Thank you."

"Happy to help."

Her pulse launched into a flat-out sprint, and she clenched her teeth in chagrin. He was only offering as a friend. And besides, if it was an offer of more, her answer would be a firm no. This was the man who had shredded her heart with the efficiency of a meat grinder. And on top of that...even if she was willing to risk her heart to him again, there was no doubt that a guy like Reece deserved a woman who didn't come with so much baggage. Accepting his help would only complicate matters. So what was she thinking?

She wasn't. That's what. It was her exhaustion doing the thinking for her. She would just have to be doubly on her guard, that was all.

Reece eased to a stop in the space in front of her

building, an old two-story house which had been converted into four apartments, two up and two down.

So he had remembered where she lived.

He hopped out and jogged around to her side to get Alyssa. "I'll get her for you."

Since she didn't know how she would have managed to haul Alyssa and the big car seat all the way up the narrow staircase with her numb finger that resembled a mini banana, she only stepped back and thanked him. "I'll get the car seat."

When they stepped into her living room from the upper hallway, Reece paused and looked around.

As Marie set the car seat into the small coat closet, where it would be out of the way for the moment, she followed his gaze around her apartment.

She'd never had a lot of money, and her tastes tended toward shabby chic. She'd repurposed an old, straight wooden ladder, painted white and distressed, into a bookshelf along one wall. Several of Alyssa's books lay in a catawampus heap toward one end. An old window-paneled door, which she'd converted into a mirror with coat hooks along the bottom, hung just below the shelf. Even though she liked the scuffed-paint look she'd given the piece, Reece probably only saw scratched-up junk as he hooked his Stetson on one of the hooks.

The two white wicker chairs were cushioned with pillows she'd made from old jeans—she'd found both the chairs and the jeans at a garage sale and been hit with the inspiration for the project. And the loveseat which sat against the living room's one blue wall had come from Goodwill. One of the cushions had been torn, but she'd duct taped it closed and then sewn a couch cover from white flat sheets. Two more of the jean pillows lay on the floor near the TV. Alyssa must have forgotten to return them to their place this morning before they left for the store.

Marie hurried to pick them up. “Uh...Alyssa’s room is just through here.” She tossed the pillows onto the couch and hustled down the hall, pushing open the door to Alyssa’s room and kicking aside stuffed animals in a path to the bed. She pulled down the blankets.

Reece gently deposited Alyssa against her pillow and stepped back.

Since it was such a warm day, Marie just pulled the sheet up over Alyssa and then turned for the hallway. But Reece hadn’t backed away more than a couple steps, and she almost barreled into him. She sucked in a gasp of surprise. But he didn’t seem to take notice. His attention roamed the room, taking in the eclectic array of crackled pink decor.

Marie pressed her lips together. The only thing she’d actually spent any real money on in this room was the mattress her daughter slept on. Everything else from the dresser to the headboard had been either a gift or ten dollars or less at garage sales or thrift shops. Even the paint in browns and pinks that she’d used to paint and then distress the bed and dresser had been in a free pile at a garage sale. She couldn’t tell by Reece’s expression whether he liked the look or not.

And why, oh, why did she care whether he liked it in the first place? Marie cleared her throat.

The sound seemed to jolt him into action, and he led the way back to the living room.

He unhooked his Stetson and fingered the brim, studying the décor in the room once more before pausing to assess her.

She rested her hands on the back of one of the

wicker chairs and tried not to let her fingers fidget with one of the shaggy seams on the denim pillow. To no avail.

Reece's gaze softened, and then warmed, and then twinkled. "It's really nice to see you again."

Drat her misbehaving heart. She swallowed. And instead of saying it was nice to see him too and shooing him out the door like she should, her mouth opened and offered, "I'm sorry to hear about your dad. Let me know if there's any way I can help."

He tapped the brim of his hat against his Levi-clad thigh, his eyes boring into hers. "You're different."

She chewed the inside of her lip. So he'd noticed. That ought to give her some measure of comfort. She dipped her chin in a nod.

She really had changed since he'd last seen her. Gone was the nurture-starved girl-woman who'd been looking for love in all the wrong places. Offering her body to—even throwing herself at—any man who would have her (or wouldn't have her, in the case of Reece), in hopes of fulfilling the craving, the gaping need, the itch nothing seemed to be able to scratch. "I finally found the love I'd been searching for in all the wrong ways."

"Alyssa mentioned a Mr. Jackson. Please tell me that isn't Dan Jackson?"

Marie tilted up her chin.

Dan had been the consummate playboy in high school. If there was a party, Dan was there and likely had a hand in planning it. But he'd done a lot of growing up in the past four years and was a different guy now. He even came to church with her most Sundays. So what if he had some things in his past he was still dealing with? Heaven knew, she did too. Dan was good for her, and she was good for him. It was just easier to remember that when she wasn't looking into a pair of green eyes flecked with amber and wanting to run her fingers over the indentation in dark curls caused by one black cowboy hat. "Yes, Dan Jackson. He's different than you remember him."

Reece tapped the hat against his leg again, and a furrow formed between his brows. "So you found the love you'd been searching for with Dan Jackson?"

A laugh popped loose before she could stop it. She scooped a hand back through her hair. "No. I meant Jesus." Come to think of it, Jesus would probably want her to make a few things right with Reece. She glanced down and didn't even try to stop herself from fiddling this time. "Reece, I really owe you an apology. That night when I...when I..." She clenched her eyes shut.

Visions of her younger self pressing her body hard against his as they lay on the warm beach sand at dusk. Of her fingers undoing the buttons of his shirt and gliding over the firm warmth of his torso as she kissed him passionately—*Stop*.

Her face felt like a frying pan ready to sear a steak for the umpteenth time today. "Reece, I'm very ashamed of many things, and that night with you is one of them. I hope you can forgive me. I'm trying to learn to lean on Jesus' forgiveness and learning to forgive myself. And I want you to know I totally understand now why you broke things off the way you did. I must have...repulsed you."

He chuckled, low and raspy.

Her gaze flew to his.

"You remember the story of Joseph and Potiphar's wife, Marie?"

He was changing the subject? She frowned but gave a little nod.

"I can tell you from personal experience he ran because he was tempted as all get out to give in." With that, he tipped his hat back onto his head, lifted his chin to peer at her from under the brim, and then offered a wink just before he opened the door. "I'll be by at nine thirty to pick you up." Her door clicked shut behind him.

Marie's legs gave out, and she sank to her knees on the floor.

Her thoughts returned for just a moment to the night so many years ago. The night Reece had left his shirt in her hand and quite literally ran to his car and left her in the sand alone. He'd texted her the next day to say he couldn't see her anymore and had been only distantly friendly to her every time she'd seen him after that. Every time until this one.

Oh boy. She scooped the fingers of her good hand through her hair. This day was not going as she'd planned.

Chapter 4

Reece changed out of his blood-stained jeans and washed up, then started bringing in the bags of groceries from the truck. He set the last of the bags on Mom's counter and swiped his finger into the bowl of cream cheese frosting she was spreading on his favorite carrot cake.

Without hesitation, she swatted the back of his hand with her spatula. "Reece Cahill, I taught you better!"

He grinned and unrepentantly stuck his finger into his mouth. Just like old times.

Well...except for the hospital bed sitting in the living room. But he wouldn't linger on melancholy thoughts right now.

"Mmmmm. Good stuff." He turned and cleaned his hands at the sink. "Listen, I'm going to check on Dad, then I have to run some groceries back into town, but I'll be sure to be here by five thirty for tonight's big shindig, alright?"

Mom eyed him speculatively. She never was one to miss a thing. But she didn't pry, only said, "Why not bring her, whoever she is, to the barbeque tonight. I'm sure your father would love to meet her."

He hightailed it from the kitchen and her prying

eyes without responding. What would Mom say if she knew he'd bumped into Marie again? She'd never been thrilled by the fact that he'd dated her in the first place. And had been vocally relieved when he'd announced he'd broken up with her. But if he were honest, he'd have to admit that he'd never quite gotten over her. And now, maybe he wouldn't have to... He swallowed at the dryness the thought put in his mouth. He needed to take things slow, but his heart had nearly tripped over itself in excitement when Marie had said she'd found the love she'd been searching for all her life in Jesus. And she'd laughed about it being Dan—that had also been a relief.

He stepped quietly into the living room. Dad's head had slipped off his pillow and was canted at an odd angle. The TV still played a very grainy version of an old *Bonanza* rerun. Reece adjusted Dad's head more comfortably onto the pillow and lowered his bed a little, then clicked off the TV. Softly, he dropped one hand onto Dad's shoulder and squeezed. What were they going to do about running Serenity Shores when Dad passed? Reece pressed his lips together and pondered their options. There were really only two. Either they needed to sell, or he needed to move back home permanently to help run the place. There was no way Mom could do it on her own.

And Mom's heart wouldn't be in selling.

Running this place with her wouldn't really be so bad. Especially not with one beautiful brunette and her cute little girl just across town. Thinking of Marie reminded him of the new cabins Dad had built along the little bluff overlooking the ocean last year before he took so sick. The minute he'd seen how she'd decorated her place, he'd thought of those bare little cabins and the potential Marie could bring to them.

Mom did a great job of helping Dad run this place, but she was more function over beauty. She kept the books and made sure all supplies were kept in stock. That, and her cooking. Her cooking was to die for.

Surprisingly it had been Dad who thought of several of the little aesthetic touches around the place. Dad was the one who'd taken the old red canoes and turned them into flowerbeds under the front windows. He was the one who'd thought to add the gazebo at the far corner of the lawn overlooking the beach, and had even draped fishing nets and tackle along the outside to make it look like it belonged.

Unfortunately, Reece took after Mom more than he did Dad in that area. And if they were going to bring those cabins up to their potential, they were going to need some help.

But all those thoughts were a bit premature. He studied his dad's face. So thin and sunken and gaunt. The doctors had said any day now. But miracles still happened, right? He couldn't just go on planning like Dad wouldn't be here, could he? And yet...he must go on planning exactly in that vein.

Dad pulled in a shuddering breath and mumbled something unintelligible in his sleep. It was so hard to see him like this. The man who'd always been so strong and vital. The man who never even retired until the cancer took hold of him at seventy-five. Even though he'd been older when Reece was born, Reece couldn't remember a day when he hadn't admired his dad's strength. Even now his strength showed through in a different way as he bravely battled a disease which was slowly sucking the life out of him. He was glad Dad was getting some sleep this afternoon, because when the guests started arriving for the welcome-home gig Mom had put together for him, the man was going to insist on sitting up and visiting, and he wouldn't get much rest.

Reece glanced at his watch. If he wanted to get Marie's groceries to her and make sure she'd been able to get to the pharmacy, he'd better get going. Mom would clean his clock if he wasn't back on time.

He poked his head back into the kitchen. "Dad's resting fine. I'll be back in a couple of hours."

Mom was humming as she put groceries away. "That's fine, dear. Don't rush. Kylen Sumner said he'd be happy to man the grill for me tonight so you can mingle with the guests. Did you get the pickles?"

"Pickles!" Reece cringed. "There's a reason why I forgot the pickles. And it's a good one too."

Mom raised a quizzical brow.

Reece snapped his fingers and pointed in her direction. "But it's a bit of a long story. I'll run by Thrift and Save and buy them on my way back tonight."

Snagging his hat off the peg by the door, he slid it on and jogged to his truck. Marie had had a few cold things in her cart, and he hoped they would still be fine by the time he got them back to her. He would have just dropped them by on his way out to the house, but he knew Mom had needed some of their groceries for her preparations for tonight's menu, and Marie's place lay in the opposite direction of Mom and Dad's.

When he arrived at Marie's door a few minutes later carrying her three small bags of groceries, he was surprised to find her door wide open. The door to the apartment across the hall—the only other apartment on this level of the old refurbished house—was open also, and some fairly loud music blared out. He wondered if Marie had to put up with the noise often. "Hello?" He poked his head inside her door.

Alyssa sat on the living room floor watching Bugs Bunny. She turned to look at him, and her eyes lit up. "Hi!"

He grinned. "I brought your groceries; is your mom home?"

Alyssa pointed across the hall. "Mr. Meyer askded her to paint that 'partment so's new people could move in."

"Oh, I see. Well, do you think it would be okay if I came in and put your groceries away?"

Alyssa squinted and cocked her head. "Are you a stranger?"

Careful, Reece. The last thing he wanted to do was teach the little girl it was okay for her to let men she'd only just met into her house. "You know what? I kind of am, aren't I? Tell you what. I'll just leave these right here by the door and go find your mom, okay?"

Alyssa shrugged and turned back to the TV. "Okay."

Reece poked his head into the other apartment. It was totally empty and smelled like fresh paint. The music seemed to be coming from the first bedroom down the hall to the left, so he followed the sound.

The sight that greeted him so captivated him that he planted one shoulder into the doorframe, folded his arms, and just watched. He could see now why Marie had been wearing the paint-spattered getup this morning at the grocery store. A large tarp covered the floor, and fresh paint gleamed on every wall but the one directly across from the door. Her back to him, Marie was painting it now. But she wasn't just painting. She was *dancing* as she painted. And singing. Rather loudly, and rather well.

She lifted the paint roller in front of her mouth, her bandaged finger poking out like an afterthought. She sang with gusto as she snapped the fingers of her other hand above her head and swung her hips, then rolled a couple strokes onto the wall before dipping into the tray near her feet for more.

He grinned. He didn't know this group, but she obviously knew the song by heart, because she had the words and her moves down pat.

The song came to a close, and as the last beats blared, she spun around and tipped one wrist as though she herself were giving the cymbal its final stroke. Her gaze landed on him, and she squawked like a startled seagull and stumbled backward.

"Watch out for the—!"

Too late. Her foot landed right in the tray of white paint.

Her eyes dropped closed, and she just stood there. Not even bothering to pull her foot from the tray.

Reece couldn't have stopped the chuckle that escaped if he'd tried.

Her gaze flew to his, and she blew a frustrated breath at a strand of hair hanging over one eye even as a rueful smile begged for purchase on her lips. "Apparently I should have just stayed in bed this morning."

He tilted his head. "I'm glad you didn't. Then we wouldn't have bumped into each other at the store."

Her eyes widened, and she bent quickly to shut off her iPod and extract her foot from the tray.

That was a definite back-off-buddy-you're-freaking-me-out look in her eyes. He took a breath. Things were different. He'd have to tread with caution. Especially considering Alyssa had mentioned Dan had asked Marie to marry him, and she'd said "maybe."

Marie scraped off as much paint as she could with

the side of the tray and then placed her foot gingerly on the tarp. At least there hadn't been too much paint still in the tray. The white only coated the shoe to just above the level of the sole.

He hurried into action and grabbed up the roll of blue paper towels lying on the tarp. Pulling several off, he handed them to her.

She used the first couple to get a grip on the shoe and remove it—no easy task with the thick white bandage keeping her first finger at a stiff, odd angle—then set to wiping down the shoe as best she could. "What are you doing here?"

He handed her another towel. "I brought your groceries. I didn't want you to have to do that chore all over again tomorrow."

Her chin lifted, and she stilled for just a moment like a regal wild mustang trying to decide if it should stay and fight, or turn and flee. In the end she did neither. She toed off her other shoe. "You didn't have to do my shopping. But, thank you. I'll go get my checkbook. How much do I owe you?"

He wanted to tell her not to worry about it, but there was a certain set to her jaw that let him know he'd better not just yet. He might be in enough trouble already when she realized he'd covered her co-pay at the emergency room with his own card. "The receipt is in one of the bags."

She left her shoes on the tarp and walked out without another word.

As he watched her walk away, his focus slipped to the gentle sway of her hips above those long, athletic, brown legs. He swallowed and forced himself to look at the floor. No matter how hard he tried *not* to think about how beautiful she still was, the battle was futile.

He switched his attention to the small section of wall that still needed another coat of paint. If it sat too much longer, she would have to wait till the second coat she'd already put on it dried completely. He grabbed up the paint roller and loaded it with paint, then set to rolling over the last small section. It was a few minutes before he felt more than heard her come to stand in the doorway behind him.

"You don't have to do that. I can finish."

She was obviously used to fending and doing for herself. He loaded the roller again and glanced at her over his shoulder. "I don't mind. Painting is therapeutic. And I didn't want it to go all tacky on you. I've almost got it done." She had a checkbook in one hand, but her arms were folded and one of her shoulders was planted into the doorframe. He turned back to rolling on the paint.

"The receipt doesn't have the pickles on it."

"Yeah, I sort of forgot the pickles. I have to run back by the store before I go home to pick them up for Mom." Not that he would have put them on her tab anyhow, but he wouldn't mention that part. But suddenly he saw a way to convince her to join him this evening at his welcome-home party. He pretended to carefully check the wall for any thin spots. "So I guess if you want to pay for them, you could come with me. Then Alyssa could get her ride in my truck like I promised her while she's awake." Satisfied that the wall was coated well enough, he set down the roller and double-checked his hands for any paint. He didn't want to get any on his clothes. "But, since the store is closer to home than here, it would be easier timewise if you just came out to the house for this dinner Mom has planned. Then I can bring you home later tonight." He glanced over to see if she was buying it.

She pressed her lips together and swallowed. "I'm not so sure your mom would like that. She didn't give me an invitation."

Reece stilled and studied her for a moment. Even though he could tell she was trying to hide it, there was definite hurt in her expression. Mom wouldn't do that on purpose, would she? "Maybe it just got lost in the mail?"

Marie shook her head. "She handed them out at church. She handed Kylen and Taysia's to them while I was standing right—" She broke off and looked away, waving a hand to dismiss what she'd been about to say. "It's not a big deal."

Reece felt a heaviness weight his heart. His frustration with his mother rose several notches. He couldn't believe she'd done that. She'd handed invitations out right in front of Marie but hadn't given her one? "Well, I want you there, so come with me."

She wriggled her pink-sock-covered toe into a small tear in the tarp and didn't answer.

"Please?"

Her eyes narrowed, but humor twinkled. "You're just trying to get another person to your welcome-home party. Not enough friends left in town?"

He couldn't stop the grin that tugged at his lips. "Maybe."

A smile etched lines at the corners of her eyes. "Well, it won't work." A bit of her old familiar sass sparkled in her blue gaze. "Sooner or later you're going to have to come to grips with the fact that you really don't have any friends, Reece." Sarcasm dripped thickly from her words.

He chuckled and rubbed at a small white speck on his thumb. She was going to say no. He could feel it. He hadn't planned on telling her about the potential work just yet, but... He pushed his hat back and peered up at her from under his brows. "There's another reason I'd like you to come too, actually."

She only offered a questioning look, and waited.

"I'd like to hire you."

She jolted straight and her jaw dropped open. "No way."

He sighed. "I can understand. You're probably too busy already. It was just a thought—"

"No! That's not what I meant. I meant—wait. What do you want to hire me to do?"

He settled into his heels and clasped one wrist behind his back. "We have three new little cabins Dad built with the intention of increasing our available space for guests. I'd like you to decorate them. You could have Alyssa with you, of course, and—"

Tears sprang into her eyes.

"Whoa." He held out his palms to calm her. "It's just a suggestion. You don't have to—"

"Reece." She was smiling now but still crying.

He lifted his hat and scratched the top of his head. "I must be missing something here, Marie."

She loosed a watery laugh. "I was just"—she swept a gesture toward the still-wet wall— "praying while I painted and asking the Lord to give me a second job that would be part time and let me keep Alyssa with me while I did it." Her face turned crimson. "Before I started singing, that is." She dashed at the moisture on her cheeks. "You have no idea... Yes. I'll take it."

"You haven't heard how much I'm paying yet."

She shook her head. "It doesn't matter. And I'll work hard, I promise." She lifted her bandaged finger. "With the upcoming doctor bills—Well, anyway. Every little bit helps."

Something inside him went still at that. And he suddenly realized just why she'd been so reluctant to go into the hospital earlier today, and was even more thankful he'd paid the co-pay for her.

Was the reason she'd had so few groceries not because she didn't need more, but because she couldn't afford to buy more? His glance dipped toward her injury, and he remembered her putting him off when he'd offered to take her to the pharmacy, earlier. He'd bet dollars to doughnuts she didn't plan on picking up her prescription.

He swallowed, hating to think of her in that situation, but knowing he wasn't in a place to press for more details at the moment. He upped the price he'd planned to pay her by five dollars an hour and got back to the conversation. "Good, so, ah..." He assessed his hands one more time and then, satisfied they were indeed paint-free, looked up at her. "Would you mind coming out tonight to look them over? If you think you could have them done by the end of July, we could start renting them out August first."

"I'll have to check with Taysia on a couple of things, but I think it should be doable."

"So you'll come?" He held his breath.

"As long as you're sure your mom won't mind?" She lifted her checkbook. "I do have to pay for the pickles."

"I'm sure it was just an oversight on Mom's part. I know she won't care. She's got a lot weighing on her with Dad and all."

"Alright, if you're sure." Her eyes suddenly widened, and she glanced down the length of herself. "Do I have time to change?"

"Sure. How about if I clean up here for you while you

do that?"

"Oh, thank you." She waved a hand toward the paint tray and roller. "The head on the roller is on its last legs anyhow, and I promised myself I'd throw it away after this time, so just chuck it and the plastic liner into the Dumpster out back. You can just leave the handle, brush, paint can, tarp, and paper towels in a stack. Mr. Meyer will be by first thing to make sure I got this done, and he will pick those up then."

"Got it."

As he set to cleaning up for her, he thanked the Lord it had been easier to talk her into taking the job than he'd anticipated. Now he needed to call Justus at Deschutes Rejuvenation and let him know he wouldn't be back. At least for the foreseeable future.

Chapter 5

With her hand encased in one of the tight rubber gloves they'd given her at the hospital, Marie hurried through her shower and into a pair of jeans, her favorite blue peasant blouse, and a pair of cubic zirconium–studded flip-flops. She worked some mousse into her hair and hoped her curls wouldn't frizz too much because she didn't have time to baby them with the hair dryer. After a quick application of light makeup, she grabbed one of Alyssa's little jackets from her room and headed down the hallway to the living room.

Reece had made himself right at home. He was hugging one of the denim pillows and lying on his stomach on the floor next to Alyssa, laughing at the antics of Daffy Duck. He'd hung his Stetson on the same hook he'd used earlier that afternoon, she noted. She also noted the rugged day's worth of beard shading his jaw.

She swallowed and fiddled with the zipper on Alyssa's jacket. "Alright, you two. I'm ready."

Reece was still laughing when he turned on his side, but when he saw her, his laughter died away. He swallowed and tucked part of his lower lip between his teeth as he scanned her quickly. It wasn't the hungry, predatory look she'd received from so many men, but an assessment of such awe that it stole the moisture from her mouth.

And then just as quickly as it was there, it was gone, and he leapt to his feet and ruffled Alyssa's already mussed hair. "Ready to go ride in my big blue truck, Superwoman?"

"Yes!" Alyssa scrambled to the old TV and pushed the off button and then pressed stop on the DVD player. "Ready!"

Marie smoothed a hand of uncertainty down the side of her jeans. "Pillows."

"Pillows!" Curls bobbed as her daughter snatched up the denim cushions and chucked them at the couch. One tumbled off and she dashed after it, then crammed it into one corner with the command for it to "stay."

Reece chuckled and grabbed his Stetson, settling it on his head, and they headed out the door. But instead of going straight to Thrift and Save, he pulled into the parking lot of the pharmacy.

She fisted her hands and tried not to look as sick as she felt. The check for the groceries had taken her account down to under twenty dollars, she still had to pay for the pickles, and payday wasn't for another week. She could just deal with the pain in her finger, and the chances of getting an infection in the cut after all the antibacterial treatments they'd done at the hospital were next to nil, so she wasn't too worried about needing the antibiotics they'd prescribed. So she hadn't planned on paying for the pills. But she couldn't just out and tell Reece she couldn't afford her prescriptions, could she?

Beside her Reece leaned forward and dug into his back pocket.

She glanced over at him.

He lifted a hundred-dollar bill up between his first and second fingers and swung his chin toward the entrance. "Alyssa and I will hang out in the truck while you run in and grab your prescriptions."

She angled him a stern look. "I can't let you do that." She'd never even let Dan pay for anything for her or Alyssa. Not that he'd ever offered, now that she thought about it.

He matched her stern expression, even copying the angle of her head. "Consider it my first order as your new boss. I can't have my newest employee getting sick on the job. Look at it as an advance. I'll take it out of your first check." He winked and stretched the bill closer to her.

She glanced down and studied his hand, brown and broad with long, blunt fingers. Her focus honed in on the number in the corner of the bill.

He was offering to help her. She couldn't remember the last time someone other than Kylen or Taysia had offered to help her. She was the all-sufficient single mother who worked full-time and then some to provide for her little girl. And God had blessed her with a great boss and odd jobs where she could keep Alyssa with her.

But the thought of simply letting that self-sufficiency go, even for just a little bit, was spring sunshine after a long gray winter. It would definitely not be hard to let a man like this take care of her. But...there were so many complications. Not the least of which was that Reece deserved a woman who was more suitable for him.

So...she would compromise. She'd accept his help, but only because it was an advance against a paycheck. This was business. Slowly, she reached out and slipped the money from between his fingers, being careful not to touch him. "Just a loan, then." She glanced up to meet his perusal once more. "And thank you."

"Of course." He nodded, but there was a hint of something more in his green eyes flecked with gold. A hint of something oh so enticing.

She fled before she slipped up and revealed any of the crazy, mixed-up jumble of emotions tumbling through her. The pharmacy had her prescriptions all ready, and it only took her a couple minutes to get back to the truck. She tried to hand him the change.

He shook his head. "It will be easier to deduct a round number from your check, so just keep the change, for now, please." Reece reached into a little cooler behind his seat and handed her an unopened water bottle as he pulled out of the parking lot.

"Thanks." She tucked the bills and change into her wallet, poured the prescribed dosage of both painkiller and antibiotics into her palm, and swallowed them down, unable to deny that having her finger stop throbbing, even for a little bit, would be a relief.

After the promised stop at the Thrift and Save, where Reece even kept his word and let her pay for the pickles, Marie found herself swallowing a lump of uneasiness as he pulled to a stop in the Serenity Shores driveway fifteen minutes out of town.

She'd only been here a few times when she and Reece had dated. She'd always been a bit intimidated by the large home, even though she'd absolutely loved the eclectic décor. But it was Mrs. Cahill who'd really made her nervous. She'd never gotten the impression the woman was too pleased Reece was dating her—and with good reason, she supposed. It was no less than she deserved, right? Many of the church ladies gave her the feeling she'd never quite match up. But that was only as it should be, considering the type of person she'd been.

She tried to remind herself the only thing that mattered was that Jesus loved and accepted her just the way she was, rotten past and all. And His love was all she needed.

Still, the fact that Mrs. Cahill had handed invitations to several around her in the church foyer, while studiously avoiding her gaze, had actually hurt a little. Most of the time she was able to steer clear of Reece's mom at church, since they attended different services, but here at the bed-and-breakfast...they were bound to meet. And chances were high Mrs. Cahill was going to be far from pleased to find her crashing this party.

She swallowed. "Reece. I'm not so sure this is a good idea."

He reached over and settled one hand on her shoulder. "I would really like for you to stay. But if you want, I can try to find someone to take you home. I don't want you to be uncomfortable."

The weight of his hand was somehow comforting. There were people who accepted her despite her mistakes from the past. She was being overanxious. There was no need for someone to go out of their way to take her home. She took a breath. She could do this. Reece wanted her here. Kylen and Taysia would be here, she hoped. And Dan would certainly be here. He never passed up the opportunity for free food, and he'd told her he'd been invited.

"Mommy, are we at the party?"

Marie glanced at Reece and hoped he could see the appreciation in her eyes. She mouthed, "Thank you," before responding to Alyssa. "Yes, baby." She forced herself to undo her seat belt and climb down from the truck.

As she helped Alyssa down from her booster seat in the back, she noticed there were already several other cars parked in the drive and along the street. She recognized Kylen's red Mustang and eased out a breath of relief. So Taysia *would* be here to keep her company.

Reece appeared at her side, carrying the paper bag with the pickle jars in it.

Marie glanced from Alyssa to the clear, blue, still-sunny skies. "Is it okay if I just leave Alyssa's coat out here? I might need to get the keys from you to come get it later if it cools off too much."

"Of course. No problem." He smiled and then turned to Alyssa and waggled his eyebrows. "You ready for some food? My mom makes a pretty mean chocolate cake! And there will be carrot cake too."

Alyssa wrinkled her nose as she scrambled down from the truck. "*Carrot* cake? Yuck! I want chocate!" Suddenly she froze in her tracks, and a huge frown creased her pudgy little brow. "Mommy, do I like *mean* chocate?"

Marie couldn't help a chuckle, and Reece joined her. She rested her hand in the middle of Alyssa's back, nudging her forward. "A mean chocolate cake is just one that's really yummy is all."

"Oh!" The little girl gasped with delight. "A dog!"

Loping toward them across the lawn was a beautiful golden retriever.

Marie shook her head at the rapidity with which her daughter could change the subject.

"That's Tawny. Hey, Tawny, girl." Reece reached down and ruffled a silky ear. "Do you want to pet her?"

Alyssa fisted her little hands together uncertainly. "Does it bite?"

"No. Tawny's a very nice dog."

As if to prove his point, Tawny got right into Alyssa's face and tried to lick her.

Alyssa squealed and darted to Marie, clambering up into her arms, where she looked down to study the panting dog from a safe distance.

"Alyssa, honey, it's okay. Dogs do that. She's just trying to give you a doggy kiss." She glanced at Reece. "Sorry. She hasn't been around dogs before."

Reece shrugged and gave her a subtle wink, then bent and patted Tawny's head as he met Alyssa's gaze. "It's okay. Tawny will be here all night, and I bet she'll have you"—he reached over and pinched one of Alyssa's cheeks, eliciting a giggle—"wrapped around her wagging tail by the time the night is through. Come on, let's get inside."

Alyssa squirmed as they started to walk. "But I want to pet the doggy now!"

Reece grinned at Marie. "I remember you always faced your fears head-on, too."

Her stomach churned a little at the reminder of the time he and some of the guys from school had talked her into jumping off one of the nearby cliffs into the ocean. She'd done it once, just to prove she could, but she'd never gone back and done it again. She offered him a weak nod.

He held the bag of pickles toward her and gestured to Alyssa. "Trade me?"

"Sure." She accepted the bag and handed Alyssa off to him.

Reece squatted in front of Tawny and settled Alyssa onto one leg. "Sit, girl."

The dog obeyed, her tongue lolling and her huge brown eyes fixed solely on Reece.

"Watch me now," he said to Alyssa as he slid a hand over Tawny's head and stroked one ear. "See? She's really nice."

Alyssa still had her little hands curled up under her chin in uncertainty.

Marie wanted to reassure her, but stopped herself. Reece was doing a fantastic job of encouraging her but not pushing her too hard. And it would do Alyssa some good to get adult input from someone besides her this time. Not to mention how wonderful it was to watch the two of them together.

Reece studied Alyssa's clenched fists for a moment, then asked her, "Are you afraid to touch her?"

Alyssa hesitated, but then nodded.

"Why?"

"She might bite me!"

Reece continued to pet the dog, who had now turned her studious expression toward Alyssa but was sitting very patiently and quietly as if she understood the whole scenario. "Do you trust me?"

Alyssa shrugged.

Marie bit back a grin even as she saw Reece do the same.

"Well..." Reece slanted Marie a quick wink before focusing on Alyssa once more. "Do you think I would lie to you?"

"Lying's wrong." Alyssa gave a definitive dip of her head, but she didn't take her eyes off Tawny.

Reece nodded. "Yes, it is. And I would never lie to you. Tawny might lick you, but she would never bite you."

"Lick me!?" Alyssa leaned back hesitantly. "Why would she lick me?"

"Well. I guess it's Tawny's way of giving kisses. She only kisses people she likes. So what do you think? Do you want to pet her?"

Alyssa still hesitated.

Marie was just about to say they should move on and Alyssa could try again another time, but Reece spoke again before she could.

"How about if you stand right here"—he gestured to the spot between his knees—"and I'll help you pet her and keep her from licking you?"

Without hesitation Alyssa slipped off his leg to stand where he'd indicated. But she scooted back as close to Reece's chest as she could manage before nodding she was ready.

Marie pressed her lips together and blinked back tears. Partly because of pride that Alyssa was willing to face her fears, but more because she'd never seen her daughter take to a man so quickly before, and it was simply devastating to know she'd ruined her daughter's chances at ever having such a wonderful father a long time ago by her own stupid choices.

Not because she didn't want a guy like him in their lives, but because a guy like him deserved someone who'd served the Lord her whole life and done things right. Waited for marriage. Possessed a little more innocence than she did. Okay, a lot more.

Tawny held her head perfectly still as Reece helped Alyssa reach her little hand out to pet the soft golden coat. At the first stroke of her palm against fur, Alyssa giggled.

Reece leaned over her shoulder and peered at her. "See? Fun, huh? I'm proud of you for being so brave!"

Marie swallowed and wished her estimation of the man wasn't resprouting so quickly. She glanced around. Where was Dan, anyway? "I'll just run these pickles into the kitchen. Alyssa, stay with Reece for a minute, okay?"

A squeal of laughter was all the response Marie got from her daughter as Tawny swiped a tongue toward her face and Reece bumped the dog away with the command to stop. A grin firmly in place, Reece glanced up and gave Marie a nod to let her know they would be fine. He held her gaze for a beat, peering at her over Alyssa's shoulder, his grin fading into something more intimate.

Warmth cocooned her like one of the heated throws they'd had at the ski lodge her mother used to take her to.

She pulled in a slow breath, and it took all her willpower to break eye contact. "I'll just..." She lifted the bag and spun on one heel.

As she beat a hasty retreat for the house, she swallowed and fisted one hand. No matter how badly she was tempted to go down that road again, she must resist. For his sake. Maybe he didn't remember exactly what she'd been like? He certainly didn't understand what a pariah she would make of him to the church people if he started dating her. And she certainly didn't need all the drama which would go along with a good man like Reece showing an interest in her.

Dan was different. He'd been a lot like her. Everyone seemed content to let them have each other. She just wished she felt more for him. But love was a choice, right? She could learn to love him. And he was really good with Alyssa too.

At the thought of her daughter, Marie was reminded once again that come a week from tomorrow, she needed to have a new babysitter. Dread dropped into her stomach. What was she going to do about that? In the small town of Marinville, there weren't a whole lot of options when it came to childcare. Alyssa had been in the one and only preschool down on Main for a while, but she'd constantly gotten sick, and Marie had been so thankful when Mrs. Hernandez had said she'd love to watch her.

Marie sighed. She'd asked everyone she could think of, and no one was able to do it. She'd make a few last efforts to find someone; otherwise she was going to have to reenroll Alyssa in the preschool.

The doors to the stone entryway which welcomed everyone to the grand log home stood wide open, and Marie was suddenly second-guessing her decision to bring the pickles to the kitchen. In her hurry to get away from Reece, what if she bumped into his mother?

Cautiously, she stepped onto the natural stone slate. She paused in a moment of awe. She'd forgotten how lovely the honey tones of the well-maintained walls were. Above her a huge chandelier, made from dropped elk horns intertwined together, shone golden light onto the framed original oils of the Pacific at sunset. The entry table was one solid piece of pine with a beautiful dark grain brought out by the natural varnish. A large mirror hung above it, and Marie caught sight of her pale features.

Best she just get on with it. The sooner she left these in the kitchen and made her escape, the less likely she was to be discovered.

She remembered the kitchen lay to her right, and headed down a hallway past the large formal dining room, noting the delicious bounty overflowing on the table. Her stomach rumbled rather loudly. She pressed a hand to it and tossed a glance behind her. Still no sign of Mrs. Cahill, thankfully.

She poked her head into the large dream kitchen.

Across the wide granite-topped island, Reece's mother looked up and stilled with her hands frozen above the bowl of lettuce she was tearing. "Marie!"

Marie cringed inwardly at the aversion in her tone.

There had been no time to evade her scrutiny. *But of course.* Based on how this day had gone so far, she should have known.

"Hi, Mrs. Cahill." She was thankful her voice didn't waver as she lifted the paper bag of pickle jars. "Reece and I picked these up at the store."

Darlene Cahill's lips thinned in decided distaste. "You can set them on the corner there." She resumed her tearing, and by the caliber of her movements, Marie could easily imagine the woman visualizing the removal of her head.

It was obvious Darlene wanted better for Reece than a girl like her. Little did Mrs. Cahill know how much Marie wanted that for him also.

The jars clinked together as she set the bag down. "Is there something I can help you with?" The least she could do was offer help. After all, she could hardly fault the woman for not wanting her to be around her son.

"No. I think I'm just about done. Thanks just the same." Darlene never met Marie's eyes.

Marie rubbed her hands down the sides of her jeans. "Okay. I'll just head back out, then. Thanks for having m—everyone over. I'm sure Reece is thankful."

The woman did look up then. She gave a little snort and then resumed her annihilation of the lettuce.

Marie took the hint and left her alone.

Her stomach had clenched up so tight during the exchange Marie felt a physical pain. Reece had been wrong. His mother definitely did *not* want her here tonight. She should just find someone to take her home.

The scent of barbequed burgers and sausage links drew her through the living room toward the large French doors that led onto the back patio on the ocean side of the house.

The hospital bed in the living room halted her. Mr. Cahill looked so frail and thin-skinned. His sparse hair fanned out around his head like a halo. The patio doors were open, and he was looking out over the ocean. He must have seen her out of the corner of his eye, though, because he swung his head her way. His eyes lit up. "Marie!" Her name sounded garbled through the oxygen mask over his face, but his tone undeniably held more welcome than his wife's had. He stretched a hand out to her, and a smile lit his green eyes. Reece had definitely gotten his eyes from his father.

Marie stepped forward and took the vein-etched hand, offering a smile of her own. "Hi, Mr. Cahill. I'm so sorry to hear how sick you've become. I've been praying for you."

He waved a hand to brush away her concern. "The Lord has given me a lot of good years. Who am I to question the portal He uses to bring me home?" He kept ahold of her and tugged her closer.

Marie clasped her thumb around his and curled her fingers over the back of his hand. She leaned her elbows on the side rail of his bed. He'd always liked her more than his wife had.

"So..." He quirked an eyebrow so much like Reece often did. "You here with my boy?"

Marie tilted her head and took in the twinkle in his lively eyes. Her lips tipped into a smile. "Yes. But no."

An anemic chuckle slipped from him. "Well, since he's only been home a day, I suppose I should give it some time, huh?"

He was so sweet. Where Darlene had more often than not set her on edge, Dave Cahill had a way of making her feel like she was special and important. "Thank you for always being so kind to me."

He nodded. "It's easy to be kind to a woman I hope will one day be my daughter."

Tears pricked her eyes. She really should tell him that would never happen, but she couldn't bring herself to shatter his hopes. She bent forward and placed a kiss on his forehead. "You're so sweet."

"Hey. How is it you can always figure out a way to wrangle a kiss from a pretty lady, Dad?"

Marie's heart stuttered even as she glanced up to see Reece striding in from the patio. She chuckled and stepped back from Dave, swiping tears from under her eyes.

Reece stopped on the other side of the bed and touched his dad's shoulder. But his curious gaze remained on her. He tipped a nod toward the patio. "Alyssa is out there with Taysia."

"Okay, I better get on out there, or Kylen will have her plate full of brownies and cake."

Reece winced exaggeratedly. "She's not allowed to have cake?"

Marie chuckled. "She's already worked her wiles on you, huh?"

He held up his fingers a short way apart. "It was just a little piece."

"Uh-huh."

He smiled softly, but there was a hint of concern in his expression. "You okay?" he mouthed.

She nodded. "I'll head out and check on Alyssa."

Chapter 6

Reece couldn't help but wonder what Dad had said to elicit tears from Marie.

She paused at the foot of his bed and reached out to squeeze one of Dad's toes. "So nice to see you again, Mr. Cahill."

Dad gave her a thumbs-up.

Reece watched her step hesitantly out onto the terrace and then turned back to find Dad's knowing gaze fixed on him. "You better snap that girl up before someone else does."

Reese eased a hip onto the bed and grinned. "Still a matchmaker, huh?"

Even though levity danced in his eyes, Dad tipped his head in sincerity. "I'm serious about this one."

"Yeah? Well, things are complicated. She already has a man in her life, not surprisingly."

Dad cocked an eyebrow. "Sometimes a man has to fight for what he wants."

Reece grinned and took Dad's hand. "I'll keep your sage advice in mind. Can I get you anything?"

Dad waved away the offer.

"Are you sure? Mom made your favorite pistachio Jell-O salad."

Dad's eyes brightened. "Since you twisted my arm, I think I will have a scoop of that."

"Good. I'll get you some."

"You'll get him some of what?" Mom bustled in from the direction of the kitchen with a salad in her hands.

"Dad wants some of your pistachio salad."

Mom's countenance brightened. "Good! I'll get it for him, Reece. You go visit with your friends."

"Alright." Reece reached up to squeeze Dad's shoulder. "I love you, Dad." He didn't plan to miss a chance to tell his dad he loved him over the next few weeks.

"I love you too, son. And don't you forget it."

Reece's throat felt thick, and he stood before he got too emotional.

When he stepped out onto the patio, Dan Jackson was standing next to Marie with Alyssa in his arms. Of course Mom would have invited him. He and Dan had been on the high school basketball team together. But that didn't mean he wanted to see the guy looking all family-like with Marie and Alyssa.

He swallowed and turned to his right to avoid the sight.

Kylen Sumner eyed him from behind the grill, his focus bouncing from him to Marie and back again. But to his credit, all he said was "Hey, welcome home. Can I get you a burger?"

Reece had suddenly lost his appetite, but he nodded anyway. "Sure. Thanks for manning the grill tonight."

Kylen split open a bun and laid a patty dripping with cheese onto it. "Not a problem. You going to be around for a while?"

Reece's gaze traveled of its own volition to the living room he'd just left, and then swooped over the grounds of the place and finally landed on Marie, before he jerked it to the burger on his plate. "Yeah, it appears that way. I plan to contact my boss tomorrow afternoon to let him know I won't be back after my six months of leave are up."

"I'm sorry about your dad."

"Thanks." Reece felt a rock settle into the pit of his stomach and swallowed.

"I sometimes need help with investigating now that I've gone private. Are you interested?"

"I appreciate the offer, but I think I'm going to be a little busy around here. Feel free to ask if something comes up, and I'll feel free to say no if it doesn't work. How's that?"

Kylen nodded. "Sounds like a deal."

"Reece Cahill!"

Reece turned at the distinctly feminine voice.

Dakota Trask strode toward him, her long blonde hair swinging around her shoulders. He hadn't seen her since the day of graduation. She'd been serving in Africa with Convoy of Hope last he'd heard.

"Dakota!" He held out his hand to give her a handshake.

She spurned his hand and wrapped her arms around his neck. "You can't shake my hand, you! It's so good to see you again!"

Over her shoulder he met Marie's gaze and gestured her over. She would want to see Dakota. They'd been pretty close in high school and probably would have been more so if Marie had been serving the Lord. Marie could surely use a good Christian friend now.

He returned his attention to Dakota. "How long have you been back in town?"

"Not long, actually. I just got home last week."

As Marie and Dan walked toward Reece and Dakota, Marie felt a strange mix of excitement combined with dread. Dakota had tried to befriend her in high school, but Marie had always held her at arm's length. She was excited to see her and hoped they could be friends, but her dread came from the fact that she was looking at the exactly perfect woman for Reece.

She swallowed and stuffed the feeling back down deep inside where it hopefully would never rear its ugly head again. She had no right to care about Reece getting together with another woman. Especially not when she was walking beside a man who'd asked her to marry him only last week. Guilt pinched her heart. How could she be having any sort of feelings about Reece when she was seriously considering marrying Dan?

Dakota caught sight of them and gave a little squeal. "Marie!"

She threw her arms around Marie's neck, much to her surprise. But she recuperated quickly and hugged her back. "Dakota, so nice to see you again."

Dakota actually gave a little bounce. "I'm so happy to be home!" Her sparkling blue eyes turned toward Dan, who still held Alyssa in his arms. "And Dan! You two got married? I hadn't heard! Congratulations!"

"Uh...no."

Marie spoke at the same time Dan said, "I'm still working on her."

Marie hid a cringe. Shouldn't a woman considering marriage to a man be a bit more excited about the prospect? *I'll get there*. She just needed to give her heart a little more time to catch up with what her mind knew was a good choice.

Reece shuffled his feet, and Marie noted the bare

burger waiting for condiments on his plate. Poor guy couldn't even get a bite to eat at his own welcome-home party.

"Oh! I'm so sorry! Me and my big mouth."

Marie detected true embarrassment from Dakota and knew she hadn't made the gaffe on purpose to humiliate her as some people had in the past. "Don't worry about it. So, tell us about Africa. But why don't we all grab some food while you do?"

Reece gave her an appreciative look.

"Oh, I just loved working there. I wanted to stay, but I've been battling malaria fairly regularly lately, so they sent me home for a while for some rest and recuperation."

Marie grabbed an extra plate for Alyssa and tried not to think too hard about what perfect timing it was that Reece and Dakota had returned home at pretty much the same time.

Dakota chattered on about how fulfilling it was to serve the needy in Africa, and Marie pondered the fact that the most significant thing she did each day was take care of her three-year-old.

Yes, Reece, who had served the last several years as a counselor to troubled youth, and Dakota, who had served in Africa, were definitely perfect for each other, and it was best she remember it.

Plates filled, the group headed for one of the wooden picnic tables. Marie stuffed her and Alyssa's plastic ware into her back pocket and managed to balance both plates, two cups of punch, and the bread roll she knew Alyssa would want, but only if it didn't touch any of her other food beforehand. Dan settled Alyssa on her knees on the bench, and Marie set her plate before her and handed her a fork from her pocket. "Oh, Mom forgot napkins. I'll grab you one and be right back, okay?"

Reece started to rise. "I'll get you some."

She waved him back into his seat next to Dakota. "No. No. I'll get it. This is your party. You eat." It only took a moment to grab a few napkins, but when she returned to the table, it was to find that someone had given Alyssa the squeeze ketchup bottle. A little bit of panic swelled inside her. Alyssa could be pretty dangerous with those things! The ketchup never came out easily at first, and Alyssa always tended to use overpressure. Marie couldn't count the number of times she'd cleaned ketchup off the walls and even the ceiling one time. She rushed toward Alyssa.

But even as she did so, her daughter complained, "Mommy! The ketchup won't come out again!" Tongue held firmly between tiny teeth, Alyssa tipped up the bottle to examine it even as her little hands trembled with the force of applied pressure.

That was when the nozzle gave way. A stream of red sauce splatted in an arc across the front of Marie's blouse. Marie gave a chirp of dismayed shock and stepped back, closing her eyes. Some of it had hit her chest and slid into regions there would be no way to clean in public.

Silence settled around the table, only broken by Alyssa's "Oops! Sorry!"

Marie opened her eyes to find Reece standing, the ketchup bottle now firmly in his grasp. Dakota had disappeared, but everyone else at the table was staring at her, or more pointedly at the front of her shirt.

"Uh..." Marie held her hands out to the side and looked down to assess the damage. Oh, it was bad. She could probably pass as an extra corpse on any Halloween slasher movie, right about now. How could such tiny hands squeeze *that* much ketchup out of a bottle?

Still, she had to look on the bright side. At least it was only her who had been tagged.

Dan turned back to his plate. "That's bad." He picked up his burger and took a huge bite.

Marie's jaw jutted off to one side. She met Reece's look.

A small smile played at the edges of his mouth, and he leaned over to squeeze some ketchup on Alyssa's burger.

Dakota was suddenly thrusting a huge wad of napkins into her hands and apologizing profusely as if she'd been the one to launch the attack herself.

Reece set the plastic bottle far from Alyssa and then stepped over and took Marie's elbow. "Come on. I'll get you a shirt to change into."

Marie protested as she swiped at her shirt. "No. It's okay. Dan can just take me home, can't you, Dan?"

"But, Mom! I haven't finished my hamburger yet, and I want cake and ice cream!"

Dan frowned. "Why do I need to take you home? It's just a little ketchup. Can't you drive?"

Dakota's eyebrows disappeared into her hairline, and her jaw dropped a touch.

Reece's face softened in sympathy. "Come on. Let Alyssa have her dinner. Besides, I still want to show you those cabins."

Just the touch of Reece's fingers at her elbow sent a wave of warmth through her. She pulled from his grasp. "Just a sec." She leaned closer to Dan, wishing he'd look at her instead of his food. "Dan, my car died today. Remember I asked you to look at it the other day because it was acting funny?"

Dan chomped on a chip. "I should have gotten to it

sooner, I guess. Sorry."

"Could you run me home in a few minutes after Reece shows me some cabins he wants me to decorate?"

His brow furrowed, Dan finally looked up at her. "How'd you get here?"

"I gave her a ride," Reece said. A ripple of something dark crossed his features.

What was he upset about? Maybe he just wanted to eat his food and was tired of waiting on her. So instead of pushing for Dan to agree to take her home, she said, "I'll be right back. Can you watch Alyssa for a sec?"

Dan had his burger three-quarters of the way to his mouth and only nodded and grunted.

Hands on his hips, Reece kicked at the ground. But as soon as he realized she'd faced him once more, he stretched a hand toward the house, and she stepped out.

The hand he rested at the small of her back felt natural, familiar, desirable.

She picked up her pace to put a little distance between them.

Reece seemed to take the hint and kept his hands to himself. Inside, he led her past his father, who'd fallen asleep, and down the hallway to his room.

Marie paused on the threshold. After all her years of promiscuity, she'd promised God never to walk into a situation that might even look promiscuous. It was her pledge to prove her changed heart.

Reece's bed was unmade, and a pile of dirty clothes lay in a heap in one corner. He pulled open his dresser drawer, rummaged around, and came up with a T-shirt that had to have been his back when he was a lot less built. It was turquoise with a surfboard company emblem on the front. He held it out. "It's old. But might fit you better than any of my newer ones."

"It will be fine. Thank you."

He nodded and pointed. "Bathroom's the first door down the hall to the left, there."

It only took her a few minutes to change and clean up. When she came back out, Reece waited for her with a plastic bag. "Thought you might want to put your shirt in here."

She'd rinsed the blouse and was thankful for a place to put the wadded-up wet material. "Thanks."

He grinned. "You're swimming in that thing."

She glanced down. The shirt he'd given her was much too large, but she'd done the best she could, tying a knot in one corner to make it look less like a bag. She grinned at him and smoothed a self-conscious hand over it. "What? I thought I looked like I belonged on the cover of *Pretty Citizens*."

His expression turned serious as his perusal roamed her face. "You do."

She held her breath, not quite able to break eye contact.

He stepped closer and tilted his head, reaching out to touch her arm. His thumb stroked softly over the skin by her elbow. "We're friends, right?"

She offered a tiny nod.

"So I hope you won't take offense when I ask...why are you with him? It's obvious you deserve someone who cares for you more." He studied her features, his eyes soft and tempting.

She held her breath. Every thought she clutched for was only a blank screen.

His focus leisurely skimmed from her hairline to her brows, brushed her lids, swept across both cheeks, and finally paused at her lips. He took half a step closer, one side of his bottom lip caught between his teeth.

Her stomach lurched as surely as it would have if she'd been free-falling on a roller coaster. Mouth dry, she slowly stepped back from him. She wouldn't do this to Dan. She wouldn't let Reece do this to himself. No matter how tempted she was.

If there was one thing she knew and understood, it was men's desires. She knew the expression on his face. He was falling for her. Only this time she hadn't worked hard, thrown herself at him, or used her body to solicit his attention. And maybe that, more than anything, terrified her.

She'd promised God she wouldn't be that way anymore. Consigned herself to settling for a man she didn't feel much for, because she never wanted to be that lost girl so hungry for just a little touch of love she would give her body to see it. And Reece could so easily make her lose her fragile control.

God's love was enough, she reasoned. She'd just have to do her penance for all those years of promiscuity. Do her part to protect Reece from himself.

Thankfully Reece didn't step after her, but he hooked his thumbs into his Levi's and stood in such a way that he blocked her route of escape down the hall. "I can see just by looking at the two of you you're not in love, so why would Alyssa say you're considering marriage to him?"

Marie lifted her chin and fiddled with the plastic bag. "Not all love looks the same. And I suppose she said so because I am."

He slid nearer and tipped his head. "And if another guy came into your life? One who"—he cleared his throat and bobbed his gaze to the floor and then back to her—"wanted to take care of you and get to know you better? One you might be interested in because you were interested in him once before...would such a guy have a chance?"

Marie's eyes widened, and she willed down the panic rising in her chest. Her mouth was drier than the top layer of beach sand on a sunny summer day.

She shook her head, backing up till her shoulder blades pressed into the wall behind her. "No, because that guy would realize a woman like Dakota is much more his type and he'd be much better off with her."

"Marie..." There was a hint of chastisement in his tone, and he reached for her hand.

She jerked away and clenched her jaw. "Reece!" She fumbled for words. "No. There would be no hope." The lie tasted bitter on her tongue. She held out one finger. "Dan and I might not have the most conventional of relationships, but we're doing the best we can. And—" She cut off before she could blurt out it was her due to live in a loveless relationship for the rest of her life.

A glimmer of something hard touched his eyes. "And what?"

"Nothing."

"Nothing?"

"Reece, please. I need to go check on Alyssa." It was an excuse, and she could see by the expression on his face he knew it.

But he stepped out of her way and stretched a hand down the hall. As she brushed past him, he took the plastic bag from her.

"I'll take this out to the truck. Then I'd like to show you those cabins and get your thoughts."

"Sure. I'll meet you at the table?"

"Be there in just a minute."

She left him as quickly as she could without making it look like she was running from him. Which she was.

The man made her pinky finger feel more than her entire body felt around Dan, and that wasn't good. Not good at all

Chapter 7

When she got back to the table, Dakota was there with Alyssa, but Dan was nowhere to be seen. A surge of anger curled through her. Where was he? She'd asked him to watch Alyssa. And he'd never given her an answer about taking her home.

Dakota was teaching Alyssa a hand-clapping chant, and they were both giggling together.

Marie eased down in front of her untouched plate.

Dakota looked over and smiled, flickering a glance to Reece's T-shirt for only a moment before her focus returned to Alyssa.

"Where's Dan?" Marie twirled her fork in the fluffy green pistachio salad mound.

Alyssa shrugged. "He askded me to stay here and went away."

Dakota offered a wrinkled nose of sympathy. "He did ask me to stay with her, if that helps. But I'm not sure where he went."

"I'm sorry, but thanks for staying with her. Feel free to mingle now."

Dakota tapped Alyssa on her nose. "Actually, we've been having a blast, haven't we, Alyssa?"

"Kota's fun!" Alyssa nodded emphatically and spoke

around the large bite of burger in her mouth.

"Don't talk with food in your mouth, please." Marie felt exhausted. She really just wanted to go home.

"Everything alright?" Concern traced the edges of Dakota's question.

Marie forced a smile. "Yes. Fine. Just been a long day." She needed to deflect the attention off herself. "Your work with Convoy of Hope sounds like it was very rewarding. Are you glad to be home? Or still wishing you were back in Africa?"

Dakota traced the grain on the tabletop. "A little of both, I guess. I love my work, and miss it. But it's been nice to see Mom and Dad again. And I really did need some rest. I feel like I've done hardly anything but sleep since I got here."

Marie smiled. "Well, I'm glad you are home for a bit."

Dakota reached over and clasped her hand. "I have a feeling we're going to be great friends."

Something went soft inside Marie. She didn't have many friends. Taysia was her best friend, but she was more like a sister, really. "I'm sorry I wasn't more welcoming back in high school."

Dakota made a dismissive sound. "We all had a lot of growing up to do."

Dakota was being kind, but Marie just smiled and was thankful for the beginning of a new friendship.

Then a thought struck. Maybe the woman could be the answer to her prayers? Marie tasted the salad, debating whether to forge ahead, then decided she had nothing to lose. "Dakota, do you have a job yet?"

Her eyes sparkled. "Yes, actually. I'll be working at a local battered women's shelter this year."

"House of Hope?"

"Yes. Why do you ask?"

Doing her best to curb her disappointment, Marie waved her off. "You'll be perfect for that job. Starting next Monday I'm going to need a sitter. The woman who's been watching Alyssa is moving. But I'll figure something out."

Footsteps sounded from behind her. "I'll watch her till you find something more permanent."

Marie's stomach dropped at the familiar masculine voice.

Reece slid onto the bench between her and Dakota.

If he watched Alyssa, she'd be forced to see him every day. His knee brushed hers, and a pleasant sensation curled through her. *Would that be so bad?* She gave herself a mental shake. "Oh, I couldn't ask that of you. You're going to have plenty to do around here. The last thing you need is a little girl to watch."

"But I want him to watch me, Mommy! Me and Tawny can play together all day!"

Marie glanced over to see that all Alyssa's fears where the dog was concerned had apparently vanished. She was currently standing next to the panting golden retriever with her arms wrapped firmly around its neck.

"It'll be fine," Reece assured.

Marie chewed her lip, studying him. "I can only pay minimum wage."

He rubbed a finger over the stubble on his upper lip. "I'll take it out of your paycheck."

There was a way he wouldn't have to pay her at all! Excitement bubbled up in Marie, and before she could stop herself, she blurted, "We could just trade. I'll decorate the cabins for you in exchange for you watching her while I'm at work. And in the meantime, I'll keep looking for a better solution."

Reece's jaw jutted out to one side. "I think

decorators normally get paid a lot more than babysitters."

"Maybe, but I'm by no means a professional decorator."

He winked. "And I'm by no means a professional kid sitter."

She laughed. "You're sure you want to do this?"

"Absolutely."

Taysia and Kylen dropped onto the bench across the table just then.

"What's going on?" Taysia asked.

Dakota's eyes lit up. "Reece is going to watch Alyssa for Marie in exchange for some decorating to the Serenity Shores cabins."

"Nice." Taysia eyed Marie's "new" shirt with a bit of a frown, but when Marie pointed from Alyssa to the ketchup bottle to her shirt, Taysia's brows rose in understanding, and she covered the mirth which sprang to her lips with the fingers of one hand.

Marie gave her the meanest fake glower she could muster and stuck out her tongue.

Taysia morphed her features into a look of pretend shock.

Marie grinned. And that's when she noticed Reece sat, hat pushed back, frozen with his cold burger halfway to his mouth, watching them with amusement dancing in his eyes.

Heat filled Marie's cheeks, and she concentrated on her plate and eating for the next few minutes.

Reece had barely downed half his burger and a couple bites of salad when partygoers started stopping by to greet him and say how happy they were to have him home again. Most of them also included Dakota in their comments to the point that Marie was getting annoyed until she reminded herself that she had just said the very same thing to Reece only minutes ago in the hallway. Everyone else was only seeing what she'd already seen. Dakota would be perfect for Reece.

She swallowed and forced down another bite of her burger.

She was glad for the distraction Kylen and Taysia offered as they visited with her. Kylen's new PI business was going well, even though it took him away from home sometimes for days at a time.

Partway through their conversation, Kylen and Taysia put their foreheads together, and for a few moments it was like she didn't exist. They both seemed happy and still so in love at times like this it made Marie's heart ache to see them together.

She glanced away and caught Reece looking from her to them and back, even though he was having a conversation with Blaine Pittman and Sophia Clinesmith.

Blaine had been Reece's youth pastor for years, and she'd heard he'd been seeing Sophia lately, hard as that was to believe.

Remorse immediately seized her. Who was she to talk?

Sophia had given her heart to the Lord not long after Marie had, and there had been a definite change in her life. And in a small town like Marinville, Marie knew from personal experience how hard it was to be liberated from who you were in the past.

Lord, forgive me. She rubbed her forehead. *I of all people have no right to think such things about her. Help her and Blaine to be happy together.*

Blaine was holding Sophia's son by the hand. Marie had heard his father had been killed in a car accident a couple years before. He was only a little older than Alyssa.

Taysia and Kylen stood. “We’re going to help clean up.” Taysia squeezed her shoulder. “See you tomorrow. Ky and I are on preschool duty.”

“Oh, okay. See you then.”

After Alyssa got a small piece of cake and ice cream, a pen and paper kept her happily drawing stick figures.

Marie felt out of place waiting so long for Reece, but since Dan had disappeared, he was her ride home, and he still needed to show her the cabins he wanted her to work on. She hoped she would be up to the task of decorating them.

As she waited for Reece and Dakota to finish chatting with the elderly Mrs. Murton, who lived down on Second, she turned her gaze to the never-ending surf that battered at the shoreline. Large rocks, some of them the size of houses, broke up the flat flooring of the water, and atop one a large sea lion sunned himself.

She certainly wouldn’t lack for decorating inspiration in this place. She supposed they were all rather spoiled by such vistas around here. The sea lion lowed and turned over, and Alyssa didn’t even lift her head. Especially during the summer, the colony that lived offshore was a common sight.

Finally Mrs. Murton said her good-byes, clutched both Reece and Dakota’s hands, then tottered off. Her ancient Cadillac would be parked somewhere along the street in the shade with all the windows rolled down so her Pomeranian would be comfortable. He never jumped out, and no one ever dared reach into the car. The dog might be small and old, but the couple of teeth he had left could still draw blood quicker than a surgeon’s blade.

Dakota said something quietly to Reece, and he responded in kind. Did Dan ever talk to her like that? Marie wished he would have at least let her know where he was going.

She pressed her lips together and tried to focus on the undersea picture Alyssa was drawing and make herself invisible. She didn't want to get in the way of whatever was building between them as they talked quietly.

Okay, that was a lie. She bit the inside of her lip. She *shouldn't* get in the way of it.

Marie realized with a start that Alyssa had drawn the scene in the bay, but with the sea life underwater also showing. It was a bit crude, but she could see the rocks in the bay, the lump she assumed was the sea lion, and even a passable likeness of the driftwood log she could see down the beach a ways—but Alyssa had drawn it floating on the water. Her undersea creatures included a couple of chubby fish and a starfish.

Marie was kind of impressed. But it was probably just her mother pride shining through. She rested a hand on Alyssa's head. "Your picture's really nice, honey."

Alyssa beamed. "Maybe Mr. Reece will want to put it on his fridge!"

"I sure will!" Reece twisted on the bench and gave his attention to Alyssa.

Marie looked up to see Dakota gathering her things.

"Bye." Dakota waved with a friendly smile.

"Bye. And if it's alright, I'll call you to talk sometime later this week?" She held her breath, knowing the offer of friendship was coming a little too late from her.

But Dakota beamed and gave her a thumbs-up. "Sounds good." The slim blonde bustled across the lawn, and Marie wondered if she did anything slowly.

She looked back to find Reece studying her from beneath the brim of his hat.

She blinked and returned her attention to Alyssa's work in progress, but she could still feel him studying her. She looked up again. "What?"

He held his silence for a beat, but the studiousness around his eyes softened. Finally he answered, "Just enjoying the view."

Even though her face heated, she pretended to misunderstand him. She turned her focus toward the panoramic vista before them. "You really do have a great view from here."

He made a sound, half grunt, half humor, but only said, "Where's Dan?"

She shrugged. "He may have had to rush off to work." Which she highly doubted, but hoped it didn't come through in her tone.

"I see." He said it like a whole world of understanding had just been opened up to him.

Marie wanted to argue that no, he didn't see. That she and Dan didn't have any problems. But since she knew that wasn't really true, she instead let it drop. "So...I need to get Alyssa home to bed here soon. Can we look at the cabins now?"

"But Mommy! I'm drawing!"

"I know, honey. Bring your paper and pen. You can draw some more up at the cabins."

"Okay." Alyssa sighed as though she was making a big concession for them.

Marie pressed her lips together and noticed Reece doing his best to hide a smirk as well. Marie rested a hand on Alyssa's head as they all rose from the table. "She loves to draw."

Darlene emerged from the house to grab the last two bowls off the buffet. She rested one bowl on each hip and eyed them with concern. "Where are you going?"

Reece seemed to ignore her question. "Mom, did you even get a chance to eat?"

Her lips pursed, and her gaze darted to Marie and then back to her son. "I'm fine. Where are you going?"

Reece directed a thumb Marie's way. "Marie is going to help me get the cabins finalized so we can start renting them next month."

"And I'm gonna draw!" Alyssa held up her pen and paper.

To her credit, Darlene smiled at the little girl. "That sounds like fun."

"In fact"—Reece squatted down by Alyssa's side and secured her attention—"how would you like to draw at the dining room table with my mom while she eats something?"

"Yay!" Alyssa dashed into the house before Darlene could offer any disagreement.

Marie started after her, but Darlene cut her off. "It's fine. I do need to eat something, and I'll enjoy her company."

Uncertainty quaked in Marie's middle. "If you're sure?"

"I'm sure." Darlene turned to her son then. "I invited Dakota for lunch tomorrow. She's a wonderful Christian girl. You should get to know her better. Please plan to be here." Darlene tossed Marie one last pointed glance and headed back toward the house.

Marie pressed her lips together and studied the ground.

Yes. She'd gotten the message, loud and clear.

Chapter 8

Reece gritted his teeth. There was no need for Mom to talk like that in front of Marie. She could try to set him up with Dakota all she wanted, but after what he'd seen of Dan and Marie's relationship, he had renewed hope that he might have a chance with her, if she would have him.

He called after Mom, "You won't mind if Marie and Alyssa join us, will you?"

Beside him, Marie hissed something under her breath.

Mom spun back toward him, and he folded his arms and waited for her response, knowing what it would be.

"N-no. That would be fine, dear."

He nodded in satisfaction. "Good. We'll plan on it, then."

Teeth clenched, he placed a hand to Marie's back and guided her toward the narrow trail up to the three cabins Dad had built on the bluff.

As soon as Mom was out of sight, Marie spun on him. "What was that all about? What if I have plans for tomorrow?"

Her blue eyes had a certain glint to them that let him know he was living perilously close to the edge. His heart rate kicked up a notch, because he suddenly realized how inviting that edge really was. In fact, if it meant getting to look into those blue eyes every day for the rest of his life, he wanted to dive off and pull her with him. Dad had said sometimes a guy had to fight for what he wanted. He would take things slow. But he was pretty sure if she had changed in all the ways it appeared she had, she was definitely going to be a woman worth fighting for. "Do you?"

"Do I what?" She threw up her hands.

He folded his arms and settled into his heels, resisting the urge to take her in his arms and confess that all the years of trying to suppress his feelings for her had vanished like smoke in the wind the moment he'd laid eyes on her in the grocery store this morning.

Heaven help him, she was beautiful.

So much for slow. A smile begged for release, but he kept it in check. "Do you have plans for tomorrow?"

"Well..." She spun away from him and shoved her fingers into her hair as she strode up the path. "No, I guess I don't."

He hurried after her. "Good. Then will you come to lunch with me?"

"Reece, can't you see? It's obvious even your mother knows Dakota is the right woman for you. She's trying to set you up. And she doesn't want me here. And she's right. Dakota is a wonderful Christian woman any man would be blessed to get to know better."

"So are you."

"I'm not available." There was a note of near desperation in her tone. Was she trying to convince him? Or herself?

He swallowed and angled himself to where he could see her face again. "I think a man should get to decide what woman he wants to spend time with, don't you?"

She picked up her pace and put her back to him again. "Yes. I suppose. But some men don't seem to know what's good for them."

He grinned, strode out in front of her, and walked backward so he could see her face. "And...you're not good for me?"

"No!" Her hands fluttered in frustration. Her next words came out much softer. "And I'm *taken*."

He pulled her to a stop as they crested out on the flat where the cabins were built. "Taken by a guy who couldn't even be bothered to help you when your daughter splattered you with ketchup?"

She huffed. "Dan's just like that. He knows I can fend for myself. I didn't need his help."

"But you *deserved* it." He swallowed the lump in his throat. She was totally missing the point. "You deserve a man who will help you even when you can do the job on your own, Marie. A guy who will drive to the store at midnight when you want double chocolate chunk ice cream. A guy who will make sure the oil is changed in your car, and keep your spare tire aired up; who will mop your floors and help you do laundry; do the grocery shopping so you don't have to after you get home from a long day at work; and get up early on a Saturday to feed the kids so you can sleep in. Not because you can't do all those things yourself, but simply because he cares enough about you to do them for you."

She glanced over, her eyes wide. She simply studied him for a long moment. And when she spoke, her words nearly pierced right through him. "This isn't a fairy tale, Reece. This is real life. And in real life you sometimes have to be happy with less than Disney-cartoon circumstances. Dan might not be all that, but he's a good guy. And...we're happy together."

"So you're saying you have absolutely no doubt Dan is head over heels in love with you? And you with him?"

She made a little noise of frustration. "Can we just take a look at these cabins?"

Fine. He'd probably pushed her too far tonight anyway. He'd give her some time to think about what he'd said. Maybe he wasn't the man for her, but he certainly knew she deserved someone who treated her better than Dan did. The guy hadn't even helped her keep her car running, for goodness' sake.

He gestured to the cabin farthest from them. "Let's start over there with that one."

The cabins were small, the largest having only two rooms, but they were made of log to match the main house and good and sturdy. Mostly finished but still empty of furniture, each had multiple decks that overlooked the ocean and beach below.

Despite the strain still looming in the air between them, Marie sucked in a breath of awe when she walked into the entryway. She took in the cedar-paneled ceiling with the skylight, ran a hand over the cherry cupboards in the kitchen, and trudged up the pine half-log staircase to examine the loft. Throughout the walk through she held her silence, but when she stepped out onto the stone slate patio at the back, she breathed out, "Wow."

He stepped up and leaned next to her at the rail.

A fog was rolling in. Far out against the horizon, all was a curtain of white, but the rocky coastline and white lines of frothy waves were still clear and sunny. Hot pink wild peas and bright yellow daisies dotted the coastline.

"These places are amazing. Your dad is a genius to have built up here."

Reece put his back to the view and leaned his elbows

against the rail, studying her face.

She had baby-blue eyes that held the power to knock the breath right out of him, long, wavy brown hair, and a pretty mouth that could drive him to distraction at the most inappropriate times. Like right now.

She cut a glance toward him, apparently having felt his study.

He kept his focus on her, knowing that, more than anything, he wanted a chance to get to know her again.

Giving a sharp little shake of her head, she strode back through the cabin. "Show me the other units and tell me what you have in mind."

The next morning Marie climbed down from Reece's truck in the church parking lot and helped Alyssa out of her car seat. Since Dan had disappeared at the party last night, she hadn't gotten the chance to ask him if he could pick them up this morning, and after that it had just seemed easier to stick with the plan and have Reece get them. Now she was second-guessing her decision. The warm feeling of completion it had given her to ride to church with him wasn't something she should be feeling.

She reached in and snagged the large Tupperware filled with the still-warm cinnamon rolls she'd stayed up late to make the night before and baked this morning.

Reece had come around the truck and now waited to shut the door for her.

"Thanks, Reece." She grabbed Alyssa's hand and hustled across the parking lot to hurry down to the preschool wing. She hoped Reece would meet up with Dakota and that she could find Dan and talk him into giving her a ride home. Maybe Reece would forget about his lunch invitation and she could escape the torture of being glared at by his mother all afternoon.

Not to mention the torture of being around Reece. His admiring looks and compliments were trying her resolve to guard her heart from his charm, and guard his heart from her mistakes.

When she'd opened her door to his knock this morning, his eyes had lit up. "Hi, beautiful," he'd said as he swept a look from her hair to her shoes and back again so quickly she might have missed it if she'd blinked.

That's when the warm fuzzies had started. And she was still trying to shake them.

He'd inhaled appreciatively and whined conspiratorially with Alyssa all the way to church about how Marie didn't care enough about either one of them to let them have a cinnamon roll early. And she'd caught herself laughing and slapping his hand as he'd tried to sneak off the lid to the container and steal a roll as he drove one handed.

So, okay, she was lying to herself again that she hoped he would run into Dakota, but it was what she knew was the right thing for him. What she *should* want.

"Mama, I'm hungry!" Alyssa tugged on her hand.

"Well, you should have eaten the cereal I gave you instead of only eating the cinnamon roll."

"What!? *She* got a cinnamon roll?" Instead of letting himself be left behind, Reece kept pace with her. He reached for Alyssa and swung her up, tickling her mercilessly. "You didn't tell me you'd already gotten one, Superwoman! Your mom wouldn't even let me *sniff* them! Now I'm really hurt!"

Alyssa giggled and gave Reece as good as she got.

"Mama must like me more!"

"What!" Reece set her on her feet. "You better run, little miss, because when I catch you, I'm going to give you a tickling you won't soon forget."

With a squeal Alyssa took off.

Reece caught her in four strides and gave her his promised retaliation.

Marie couldn't help but chuckle even as she called, "Come on, you two, we're going to be late!"

Alyssa hadn't taken two more steps before they were right back where they started. "Mama, I'm hungry."

"Honey, you just want another cinnamon roll. You'll get a snack in Sunday school and another in children's church, and we'll have hot dogs and chili when we get home."

"But I don't like hot dogs."

"Well, we'll try to get something different the next time we go grocery shopping."

"You always say that! And we still eat hot dogs and chili."

She supposed that was true. Because she always seemed to run out of money in the grocery budget. But this was not the time or place to discuss her finances. Especially not since she could feel Reece studying her with a touch of speculation and understanding as he held one of the church doors open for them. Marie clenched her jaw and kept moving.

Great. Now he probably saw them as a charity case. *But would it be so bad to be* his *charity case?* That did it. She was losing her resolve to keep him at arm's length. And that just wouldn't do. She needed space to regain her determination. How was she going to ditch him?

She needn't have worried. Reece's mom and Dakota stood chatting in the foyer, Darlene smiling and engaged in a way that showed she really liked the younger woman.

"Reece!" Darlene called, gesturing for him to come over.

Dakota looked amazing in a long gypsy skirt and beaded orange blouse that made her tan beautiful against her blonde hair.

Marie waved at her with a smile and took advantage of Reece's distraction to zip Alyssa down the hallway toward the preschool wing.

"But I wanted to say good-bye to Mr. Reece!" Poor Alyssa was practically running to keep up.

Marie slowed down. "I know, baby. But he's busy right now. We'll have to see him afterward to get your car seat. Uncle Kylen and Aunt Taysia are your teachers this month. Won't that be fun?"

"Yay!"

Marie eased out a breath of relief that her daughter was so easily distracted.

This was another reason for her to stay away from Reece. So Alyssa wouldn't get too attached to him.

After she dropped off Alyssa, she set her cinnamon rolls in the classroom where her Sunday school class would meet during the second service while Alyssa went to children's church. She took a moment to scan her notes. Even though it was only a five-minute talk, she was a bit nervous about sharing in front of the whole class. But it was tradition. Everyone who signed up to bring a treat also gave a five-minute mini devotional at the beginning of the class time. At least she'd be able to get it over with quickly. Hopefully what she planned to share would make sense and reach people. Taysia had looked it over on Friday at work and, with tears in her eyes, told her it was amazing.

Marie wasn't so sure. She chewed her lip and stuffed the paper back into her purse as she headed for the sanctuary. Sure, she'd been able to get it all down on paper, but would she be able to say all the stuff bumbling around in her heart? That was if she could even make herself get up in front of everyone when the time came. Sheesh! She eased out a breath. *Lord, I'm going to need a big kick in the seat of the pants when it's time to share, and maybe an extra helping of peace to take away these jitters would be nice too.*

The service had already started when she slid into the back pew. She hadn't had time to look for Dan, but he would probably find her once he arrived. He was notorious for being late to church. And if she didn't see him here, she would likely see him at the pickup basketball game the youth usually put together for a few minutes after church. Dan, Kylen, and Taysia were generally the ones who helped the youth pastor, Blaine, supervise the youth.

Even though most everyone was standing, she sank down onto the padded bench. She just needed a moment off her feet. It felt like she'd been rushing for forever. It had been a long week, capped off by a lot of emotional turmoil.

She closed her eyes and pulled in a slow breath, then eased it out through pursed lips. Her thoughts turned to Reece. She clenched her teeth. *Lord, I'm really going to need Your help not to be selfish for the next few weeks. Help me to remember to put Reece's needs above my own. And help Reece to see he'd be better off with someone like Dakota than with me.*

Beside her the cushion sank, indicating someone had sat beside her. A fleeting moment of thankfulness that Dan had found her disappeared as Reece's cologne registered with a pleasant ripple of awareness.

She deflated and kept her eyes closed. *Lord? Were You listening?*

Maybe He had been. Maybe this was a test.

She turned her gaze on Reece. He was singing, but gave her his attention and quirked a brow as though to ask what she wanted.

He looked different without his Stetson. She'd forgotten how curly his hair was. He had it trimmed close on the sides and a touch longer on the top. Just mussed enough to invite the combing of her fingers. She fisted her hand.

Leaning closer, she whispered, "Dan usually sits by me."

"If he shows up, I'll move," he whispered back.

"What if he shows up and sees you here and gets the wrong idea?"

"If he doesn't boot me out of the way, he doesn't deserve you. He better learn to fight for what he wants."

An elderly lady in front of them turned and shushed them with a scowl.

Reece leaned even closer and spoke right into her ear. "Like I am."

Marie snatched up her bulletin and dug in her purse for a pen. "What about what I want?!?" she scrawled, giving "I want" three quick underlines. She thrust the paper at him.

He read it, then reached over and took the pen from her hand. "What do you want?" He'd underlined the word "do."

Marie felt a surge of anger so forceful she almost hucked the pen he handed back to her across the sanctuary. What did *she* want? She stuffed the pen back into her purse and shoved the bulletin into the case on the iPad Kylen and Taysia had given her last Christmas.

What *did* she want?

She wanted everyone to be happy. That's what. Alyssa. Reece. Dan. Darlene. Dakota. *Myself.* The problem was, there didn't seem to be a way to make everyone happy in this situation.

But if making others happy curtailed her own happiness a little, so be it.

Now if only the stubborn man beside her would just open his eyes and see what was best for him.

Chapter 9

Marie swallowed hard and smoothed her hands over her skirt as Brad Tolland, the leader of their Sunday school class, closed the opening prayer.

He scanned the room and smiled brightly. "Before we get into today's lesson, we are privileged to have Marie Sinclair bring us our Sweet Inspirations segment this morning."

Marie stood on jellylike legs. She was glad she hadn't given in to the temptation to eat one of the cinnamon rolls this morning as she pulled them out of the oven, or someone on the front row would likely soon be wearing it.

Breathe. Just breathe.

Thankfully Reece had been called away by his rather perturbed mother just after the main service had come to an end, and Marie had cut and run for this room without him following. She'd be even more of a nervous wreck if he were in the room, because he, of all people, knew intimately some of the journey she planned to share.

She stopped behind the much-too-skinny podium, smoothed out her notes, then white-knuckled the edges. She forced a smile and eye contact. "Good morning, everyone. First, I'll ask you to say a quick prayer for me—and for yourselves, because I don't want anyone to leave wearing my breakfast."

A chuckle rippled through the room even as Marie felt her face heat. Why had she said that? It certainly hadn't been in her notes.

She glanced down at the paper. *Focus*. "Seriously, when Brad asked if I'd be willing to do a Sweet Inspirations slot, I totally didn't want to do it, but I told him I'd think about it. All that week, so many little things happened that reminded me of how far God has brought me, and I really felt this strong sense God wanted me to do this." Her gaze landed on Dakota. *A friendly face! Thank You, Jesus.* "So the next time Brad asked, I said yes...reluctantly, very reluctantly...but Brad got his yes, nonetheless."

Another chuckle. Maybe she wasn't going to bomb this as badly as she'd feared.

"For my treat this morning, I made cinnamon rolls."

"And they're great too!" Graham Sanders called from the back of the room with a full mouth.

Marie smiled as a rumble of humor spread through the room. "Thanks, Graham. Anyhow, I wanted to relate those to the woman at the well we read about in John chapter four. Cinnamon rolls wouldn't be much without the filling. If there was no butter or cinnamon and sugar wrapped up inside all the dough, they wouldn't be much to speak of. But just adding those few ingredients sort of brings them to life, you know?"

Several nodded. At the back of the room, a few people were still dishing rolls onto paper plates and grabbing coffee from the dispenser. This was casual. She could do this. She took a breath.

"Before I met Jesus, I was a lot like the woman at the

well. I'd had a lot going on in my life. Had searched for true, real, lasting love for a long time." She swallowed. "My mother chose to leave my father and me when I was ten years old for another man. I haven't ever seen her since she walked out the door. She ruffled my hair, said she was going to the store for a few minutes, and never came back. My father found out from one of her friends that she'd moved across the country with a man she'd been seeing for quite some time." Marie paused to regain her composure. "My father turned to drinking. He was in and out of jail, and I often stayed with my aunt, who resented having to take care of me. She had her own two problem children."

She met Dakota's eyes and saw so much pain there it was like a punch in the gut. She needed to lighten this up.

"Anyhow, the long story short, my dad was arrested when I was just sixteen for breaking and entering with intent to harm. He got seven years. I was on my own. My aunt said she wouldn't take me, that I was old enough to take care of myself."

Several tsks reached her ears.

Marie pressed her lips together. She was about to get to the hardest part. But this was important. *God, use my patheticness to reach someone. To keep them from traveling so far down the path I traveled*. "I was all alone and I felt so...*needy*. I had this hollow ache inside I knew I needed to fill or die trying. But I had no idea where to look."

At the back of the room, one of the blonde Blackburn twins rolled her eyes and fiddled with one of the three diamond lip rings in her upper lip. Her expression said she was having a hard time believing Marie's story. Either that or Marie shouldn't have let it control her life.

Marie pressed on despite the knot which formed in her stomach. "So I looked pretty much everywhere. I looked in drugs. But thankfully I didn't like the feeling of waking up and not being able to remember where I'd been or anything that had happened the night before. Maybe it was God's way of sparing me from that road." She shrugged. "I looked in alcohol. But again, my father had always been such a drinker booze never appealed to me much. About that time our landlord figured out Dad was gone, and he kicked me out of the house we'd been renting. That was when I turned to...men."

She felt warmth crawling up her neck. Why had she thought this was a good idea? Didn't a lot of people in the church already look down on her enough because she'd had a daughter out of wedlock?

Dakota offered a little nod of encouragement and Marie could have run over and hugged her.

"At first it was just to get a little money or have a bed to sleep in for the night. And then, it just sort of became the thing I did. I knew it wasn't right. And I knew it wasn't filling me up. But I didn't know where else to turn."

She flipped her notes over. "About that time I was walking through town when I happened to see Mom's Gym was hiring a receptionist." She laughed. "Many of you know Taysia Sumner owns that place, and I have to tell you, I have no explanation for why she hired me other than she told me years later she saw a lost soul and knew giving me a job was a way to help."

Great, now she was going to cry. "The woman at the well had had five husbands. I was like her in a way, only worse. I'd tried everything. Every guy who would have me. I was still hollow. No butter. No sugar. No cinnamon. But slowly over that first year I worked for Taysia, I saw something in her...something I knew I was craving, but just didn't quite know how to get my hands on. She started bringing me to church and got me a Bible, which I barely read."

More chuckles relieved a bit more of her tension. She was almost through.

"I was still doing my thing, but oh man, how I wanted the inner peace, joy, and kindness I saw in her. The Bible says people will know us by our love, and let me tell you, Taysia did a LOT of loving on me. She helped me get into a place and probably gave me more chances when I goofed up at work than a Dalmatian has spots. It wasn't until after I got pregnant with my daughter, Alyssa, that I finally was hit one day by what a rotten sinner I was. It took that long for my eyes to be opened. I know Taysia did a lot of praying for me. And the Holy Spirit was working on me.

"Jesus told the woman, 'Everyone who drinks this water will be thirsty again, but whoever drinks the water I give them will never thirst. Indeed, the water I give them will become in them a spring of water welling up to eternal life.'

"I have to tell you, I'd never experienced such joy, such peace, such fulfillment, as I felt in the weeks after finally surrendering my life to God. We aren't made to thirst after the empty junk in this world. All of it will leave you craving for more. And all of it is the devil's counterfeit to what God wants to give us. True satisfaction. True ecstasy. True love. The water in Taysia's life welled up and splashed over onto me, bringing me eternal life. And I hope to be the type of person who will splash a little love and joy and peace and Truth onto those I encounter. So while the filling in the cinnamon rolls isn't quite the same, I'd like you to remember the next time you eat one that the butter and sugar and cinnamon are a little bit like God's love in our lives. We wouldn't be much without it. And if we pass it around, we can make everyone we encounter a little bit sweeter. Thank you."

She'd made it. She grabbed her notes and hurried to her chair. *God, use my words for Your glory.*

Standing in the hallway near enough to the open doorway to hear Marie's words, Reece breathed deep, thankful she'd made it through. He stepped forward and peered up toward the seat Marie had just taken. He'd kept out of sight as he listened, and prayed for her as she talked, but now his heart was beating about two hundred times faster than normal. His mouth was dry. And his palms were sweaty. Because he knew he'd just been listening to the woman he wanted to spend the rest of his life with. Dan Jackson could just find himself another woman.

Marie waited for Reece by his truck after service, determined to weasel out of the lunch invitation. She recalled the way Darlene had glowered at her after the service, and shivered. Sitting through that meal would be torture.

She'd planned to use Dan as an excuse, but he apparently hadn't shown up to church today. At least, if he had, she hadn't seen him. Not even at the quick pickup game in the gym. But her salvation had come in the form of Mr. Novak. He'd ambled up to her in the foyer and mentioned he'd seen her car parked at the

Thrift and Save and asked if everything was alright. When she'd told him it died like the traitor it was, he'd offered to take a look at it for her. For free. Miracles never ceased. She'd hugged him and promised she'd meet him at her car at one o'clock this afternoon. And she'd been practicing her lines for Reece ever since.

The church's double doors opened, spilling Reece and Dakota from the entryway. Reece said something, and Dakota laughed and smacked him on the shoulder with the back of her hand.

Marie swallowed and glanced down to where Alyssa had busied herself drawing a picture on the pavement with a white chalky rock. Today she had sketched Reece's truck. Marie recognized it by the big roll bar on the top even if the wheels were slightly misshapen.

"Hey there, Superwoman!" Reece lifted a hand of farewell to Dakota as he squatted down to study Alyssa's drawing.

"Mr. Reece!" Alyssa leapt up and flung her arms around his neck.

"Whoa!" Reece caught his balance and checked out her drawing over her shoulder. "Wow, kid." He set her back and ruffled her hair. "You are going to be an artist someday."

"I like to draw!"

Reece smiled and bopped her on the nose with one finger. "And you're good at it, too. Ready for lunch?"

"Yes!" Alyssa thrust chubby arms above her head and danced like a native around a ceremonial fire, her chalk rock still clutched firmly in one hand.

Marie took a breath. "Actually..."

Reece darted her a look.

She offered a squint of apology. "We're going to have to take a rain check. Mr. Novak said he could help me with my car this afternoon, and since he's offered to do it for free, I really couldn't turn him down." Of course she didn't mention that he'd said he'd be free all week and could meet her anytime.

But there was a knowing expression on Reece's face as he regained his feet and Alyssa returned to her art project. He took a step nearer. "Mr. Novak, who retired last year and spends most of his week fishing off the pier? That Mr. Novak? And he could only meet you this afternoon, huh?"

Marie dropped her gaze to her fingernails and hoped she didn't look too guilty. But she wouldn't lie. That was another old habit she'd vowed never to return to after she gave her life to the Lord. She would just avoid the question. She swallowed and peered back up at him through her bangs. "Do you think you could give me a ride to Thrift and Save? I'm to meet him there at one."

A grin dimpling his cheeks, Reece advanced on her with such swiftness she retreated until her back was pressed to the passenger door of the blue dodge.

Her attempts to control her expression and not offer him a smile of encouragement failed. So, with both hands, she clutched her purse in front of her like a barrier.

Purposefully, he placed a palm to the glass on either side of her head, then bent down to study her face intently. His expression slowly turned serious, and he held his silence.

Her own smile fell away. She tried to focus on her purse, but her disobedient eyes kept rebounding to his every few seconds until they finally just refused her wishes altogether. She wet her parched lips.

The years had done nothing to hinder his good looks. If anything, the loss of any remaining boyishness had made him even more handsome. There were very slight laugh lines at the corners of his eyes now. And his angular jaw already showed the beginnings of the stubble he'd shave off tomorrow morning. A shock of hair had fallen across his forehead, and her fingers itched to reach up and brush it back, maybe trail over his cheek to the place his dimples had been only moments ago.

She gripped her purse more firmly.

Finally a hint of humor returned to tug at the corners of his eyes and ticked up one side of his mouth, revealing one of the dimples. "Thanks for not lying to me."

So he knew she could have met Mr. Novak anytime this week. She felt heat suffuse her face.

"I just have one question for you."

She arched her brows in question, wishing his cologne wasn't tantalizing her to lean in and inhale her fill.

"Am I really so repulsive to you that you would choose car repair over lunch with me? Or is there something here I'm missing?"

She puffed out exasperation. Why was it so hard to do the right thing here? She really didn't want to hurt him. "Reece, you are a wonderful guy. And I'm sure if things were different, I'd love to get to know you again. But there's Dakota...and Dan." She hated that Dan had come as almost an afterthought.

Reece tipped his head, and she suddenly wished he'd worn his Stetson today—to cut down on the glitter of emerald fire burning in his eyes. "Do you love him?"

Oh boy. Yet another question she needed to avoid. She glanced pointedly at her watch. "Do you mind if we get going? I don't want to keep Mr. Novak waiting."

The fire in his gaze faded into all-out humor. His left arm buckled until his forearm rested on the glass by her head, which brought him so close her skin pebbled with awareness. With his other hand he had the audacity to lift one of her curls and smooth it around a finger. His gaze drilled into hers. His movements were unhurried.

Her heart forgot that its sole job was to pump.

When he spoke, his words were a low rumble not unlike a purr. "You know the only reason I broke things off was because you weren't serving the Lord, right?" He waited for a beat, offering her a chance to reply.

But after the way his breath had warmed her cheek, she couldn't come up with a single coherent thought.

"Since that's changed, there are a couple things you should know..." His thumb stroked over her curl one more time; then he loosed it. "I'm not interested in Dakota."

She held her breath.

He pushed away from her and dug his keys out of his pocket. "And Dan is going to get a run for his money." He gave her a bold wink and then turned away, calling for Alyssa to climb in because they were leaving.

Chapter 10

I'm not interested in Dakota. Dan is going to get a run for his money.

I'm not interested in Dakota. Dan is going to get a run for his money.

Reece's words from last Sunday kept running through Marie's mind as she did chores around the house Tuesday evening. Alyssa splashed and sang happily from the tub while Marie did the dishes and wondered what she should fix for dinner.

All day she'd tried not to think about Reece's declaration. All day she'd lost the battle. He'd texted yesterday to say he was working on getting her added to their payroll and covered by their property insurance and he would get ahold of her later.

Her brow tightened when she remembered that. So he'd been serious about paying her more than she could pay him for watching Alyssa. She was torn by encouragement on the one hand that her budget might actually balance this coming month, and discouragement on the other because she didn't like to be indebted to anyone. And this felt like he was doing her a huge favor.

Thankfully Mr. Novak had been able to figure out

what was wrong with her engine, and the parts had been available at the local auto store. It had been a perfect storm of both her alternator and her starter dying at the same time and had cost her so much it made her nauseous. But she didn't know what she would have done without her car all week. And she'd baked Mr. Novak a batch of brownies out of sheer thankfulness for his help.

She grinned as she recalled Reece's piqued expression when he'd dropped her off at the Thrift and Save on Sunday. "I'd planned to work on this for you after lunch," he'd said as she'd helped Alyssa from his truck. Which she had known. That had been another reason she'd been thankful for Mr. Novak's offer of assistance. The more time she spent with Reece, the less control she had over her errant heart.

Which brought her back to the reason she was thinking about him, *again*...

His last text had said he'd see her soon, but maybe the lunch his mother had set up for him and Dakota had gone better than he'd anticipated, because she hadn't heard from him since.

She squirted soap into the dishwasher's dispenser and slapped the lid shut, angry with herself for dwelling on him for the millionth time today.

The doorbell rang and her pulse quickened. What if it was him?

She pressed start on the machine, grabbed up a towel, and dried her hands as she hurried to the door.

The peephole revealed Dan.

Relief and disappointment mingled in a frustrating mix. She eased her head against the door and gripped the towel tightly. It was so unfair that after only a few days of having Reece back in her life, he was totally consuming her thoughts and emotions. How was she going to fight this?

The doorbell rang again.

She jolted. She'd left Dan standing in the hallway. Turning the latch, she pulled back the door and smiled at him. "Hi."

He held up a pizza box and a case of Pepsi. "I brought dinner."

She stepped back and gestured him in. He'd brought dinner? *And no doubt an apology*. She hadn't seen nor heard from him since Saturday night. She hoped her skepticism wasn't too apparent in her expression.

He set the food on the table and spun toward her, arms held out for an embrace. She let him pull her into a hug but pressed a hand to his chest when he leaned in, obviously angling for a kiss. "Where've you been?" She scooted around him and lifted three plates from the cupboard. "Alyssa, honey! Time to get out of the tub. Mr. Jackson is here, and he brought pizza for dinner."

"Alright!"

Several loud squeaks and a *sploosh* had Marie cringing and wondering how much water she'd find on the floor later.

She turned to face Dan with the plates in her hands and cocked an eyebrow at him, knowing she wasn't doing a very good job of hiding her irritation.

He rubbed the back of his neck and then set to tearing open the Pepsi box. "I went camping. Needed to do some thinking."

Marie's jaw jutted to one side. "You didn't call. Not even a text."

His gaze still on the blue case, he nodded. She saw his throat work, and then he folded his arms and focused right on her. "Neither did you."

She opened her mouth to contradict him, but then realized he was right and shut it. She hadn't called him. Or texted. Hadn't even thought about it, actually. Her heart started to pound against her sternum, and she knew she must look like the proverbial deer in the headlights. She pushed herself into motion. "You're right, I didn't. I'm sorry." The plates clattered when she set them down. A frown etched a furrow between her brows.

Dan took one of the plates and set it across the table in Alyssa's spot. Then stepped over to the counter and grabbed up the roll of paper towels.

Alyssa rushed in, her nightgown on backward and askew. "Mr. Jackson!" She threw her still-damp arms around him.

"Hey, tyke. How've you been?" When he swung her up, she wrapped her legs around his torso as well. "Wow, you are getting strong!" Dan tickled her gently.

Alyssa giggled and squirmed and finally released him.

But as Dan pulled out his chair and took his seat, no humor illuminated his features.

Marie swallowed her sudden dread. Why was he here? "Alyssa, honey, sit down and let's say thanks."

Alyssa obediently scrambled into her seat and folded her chubby hands.

"Dan?" Marie deferred to him.

He nodded and said grace with a solemnity she'd rarely seen in him. She considered carefully all his actions since he'd walked in the door. Every nuance of his expressions. Each thing he had said. And with each consideration her dread mounted. He was here to break up with her.

She clenched her jaw.

Dan cleared his throat. She returned to the moment with a start. How long had the prayer been over? Her face heated.

Dan was helping Alyssa get a piece of pizza out of the box, but his gaze was on her.

She tried to offer him a smile. "I'm glad you're here."

He pursed his lips and twisted them to one side, wiping grease from his fingers onto his paper towel. "Yeah, the guy who brings dinner is always nice to see, huh?"

"No, that's not—" She suddenly had a flash image of them ten years down the road. Both of them with a few more wrinkles and pounds, sitting exactly where they were now. Alyssa would be on her phone—or whatever new device had been developed by then—and she and Dan...

She couldn't see it. She and Dan. Ten years from now. No image came to mind.

"I'm sorry. That's not what I meant." She tried to focus on eating, but couldn't seem to find any taste to the pizza.

Marie knew they couldn't have the discussion they needed to in front of Alyssa. The meal was filled with awkward silences hanging between stilted conversation.

Finally, Alyssa finished her second slice and asked to be excused.

Marie nodded. "Take your plate to the sink, please."

Alyssa hadn't been gone more than two seconds when Dan folded his arms on the table and pegged her with pain-filled eyes. "We need to talk."

She sighed. Nodded.

In the living room Alyssa's favorite DVD began to play.

"I've been pretty patient. You said you needed time.

But then...at Reece's place the other night..."

Marie's heart rate kicked up. She started to shake her head.

Dan held up a hand. "I saw the way you looked at him. The way he looked at you. Marie, it wouldn't be fair of me to keep you from that."

"Dan." She stood and hurried to his side, squatting next to him and peering up into his face. "I told him I was with you."

He reached out and fingered one of her curls. "You've never looked at me the way you looked at him."

"What are you talking about? I didn't look at him any way."

"Yeah, you did. I followed you inside to help once I asked Dakota to watch Alyssa. I saw you two in the hallway. You're in love with him and you don't even know it, Marie."

"Dan, I'm not. It's been four years since—" She batted the past away with a sweep of her hand. It was water under the bridge, and there was no sense in dredging it back up. "We can do this, Dan. I just needed a little more time." She poured every ounce of emotion she felt into her eyes. Willed Dan to believe her. Not to leave her.

He couldn't break up with her. Not now, when she needed him as an excuse to keep Reece at arm's length.

Guilt gripped her. What was she thinking? Dan wasn't some tool in an arsenal she could pull out at a moment's whim when needed. He was a man. A man she cared for. She *did* care for him. A lot. Didn't she?

Just not enough to call him when he goes missing for three days.

Her shoulders slumped. "Maybe you're right."

He stood and grabbed a Pepsi for the road, then

strode to the door and opened it slightly, but stilled and turned back to her. "I thought you'd be relieved. Even happy."

A sardonic smile tugged at the corner of her mouth. She shook her head. "No. But I think you are right, Dan. You deserve a woman who is head over heels for you. And I'm sorry to say that as much as I do care for you, I'm just not her."

His whole body seemed to shrink and sag. "Yeah, that's what I figured. I really do wish you all the best, Marie. I hope he makes you happy."

Marie started to rebuff him, but let it drop instead. Let him think what he wanted. "Good night, Dan."

He cupped the side of her face and trailed a thumb over her cheek. "Night, Marie. You take care of yourself."

"I will. You too."

He swung the door the rest of the way open to reveal Reece on the other side looking a little guilty.

Her heart did a flip. How much of the conversation had he heard?

Dan huffed a shot of air through his nose, but then turned to look right at her. "I mean it. Be happy." And with that he brushed by Reece, only offering him a clap on the shoulder and a "Good to see you" before disappearing down the stairs.

Marie's heart broke a little more. Only because she knew Dan so well could she see how much that had cost him.

Reece watched him disappear into the dark before turning back to her with a questioning look. In each hand he gripped several plastic grocery bags.

Marie felt more than a little vulnerable at the moment and was totally not ready for another battle with her emotions where Reece was concerned. Or for him to know she and Dan had just broken things off.

Had he heard? She tilted her head.

Judging by the gleam in his gaze, he'd overheard plenty.

And by the looks of all the bags he was laden down with, he'd brought more groceries than she could afford for the *month*. "Why are you here?" The question emerged with much more of a snap than she'd intended. "Sorry." She stepped back and gestured him past. "Please come in."

He deposited all the bags on the end of the table not covered by the remains of dinner, and then headed for the door again. "Just a few more bags in the truck."

"Reece..."

He didn't seem to hear her.

Marie pinched the back of her neck and examined the table overflowing with groceries. Cereal and strawberries and bread. Cookies and soda and potato chips. Yogurt and butter. Jam and several small blocks of cheese. And those were just the first four bags she peered into.

She willed down a swell of appreciation tainted with frustration and settled her hands on her hips. There was no way she could accept all this without trying to repay him. And she couldn't afford all this. He was really putting her in a spot. And she didn't have the energy at the moment to figure out how to handle it.

Reece breezed back in, and she blinked hard and spun away on the pretense of taking the leftover pizza and Pepsi into the kitchen, but he must have seen her expression, because he followed her.

"Hey," he said softly as he set the bags he'd been carrying on the floor.

She glanced down to see flour and sugar and several

packages of meat.

A little bit of anger started to smolder. How could he put her in this situation?

He took the pizza box and the Pepsi case from her and set them on the counter, then cupped her shoulders and peered into her face. "What's going on? Did Dan hurt you?" Consternation crinkled his brow.

"Dan? No." She rotated her shoulders out of his grasp and stepped back to lean against the counter with arms folded. "What is all this?" She swooped a hand over the bags by his feet, feeling her teeth grind together.

He hooked his thumbs into his belt loops and tilted his head. "This is a spur-of-the-moment gift."

She threw her hands up in exasperation. "Reece, you can't spend this much money on me! And I can't afford to pay for it."

He snatched off his hat and tossed it on top of the pizza box. "This isn't about a few groceries, so what is it about?"

She was annoyed to feel tears pricking the backs of her eyes.

"Marie..." He said her name like an embrace and apology wrapped up in one as he stepped over the bags and once more stood before her.

As if she wasn't having enough of a hard time controlling her emotions with him across the room. She put a hand out to keep him back, but the minute her fingers contacted the softness of his T-shirt, they betrayed her and simply rested there.

He touched her chin, gently raising her face to his. "Talk to me."

She swallowed, willing away the urge to throw herself into his arms and beg him to take care of her like this for the rest of his life. She tried to look away, but the power of his gaze held her captive. "You can't be here, Reece. Shouldn't be here."

With the knuckle of his first finger, he caressed smooth, short strokes along her jaw. "Why not?" His words were so soft she almost didn't hear them.

Why not? There was an answer. She should have an answer, but for the life of her she couldn't pull it from the depths of herself. "Because..." was the only lame reply she could come up with.

One corner of his mouth ticked up, and a gentle teasing light sparkled in his eyes. "Because you are still attracted to me and it scares you a little? Because you and Dan just broke things off, and now you don't have him as an excuse between us anymore?"

She swallowed. He probably didn't know how close he was to right. But there was an even bigger reason, and he apparently needed her to spell it out for him, point blank. "Reece, there's a more important reason, and you really need to consider it."

"Enlighten me." His words were serious, but humor etched the corners of his eyes.

She did push him away then. She had to or she was going to go crazy. She stalked over to the grocery bags and started thrusting stuff into the cupboards. The thing was...no matter how many times she rehearsed how to say what she was feeling, it came off sounding petty and self-deprecating. And that wasn't what she wanted at all.

How did a woman go about telling a man she wasn't good enough for him without it seeming like she was fishing for him to lavish praise on her?

Finally she forced herself to be still and just say what was on her mind. "Reece, you of all people know I've done things not to be proud of. You—you're—you've always lived for God and done what's right."

"Marie—"

"No, just let me finish."

He quieted, but there was a bulge in his jaw that told her he wasn't too happy about it.

"Dakota, or someone like her, those are the kinds of girls you should be interested in. Not me. I don't want to be the one who ruins your reputation and makes people see you in a bad light."

Reece's eyes narrowed. And his jaw worked back and forth like a bull chewing cud.

Good. Maybe he was realizing the truth she'd just spoken. She resumed putting groceries away. He continued to hold his silence, and she willed herself not to cry as she tucked items into the cupboards and fridge. She wished this hadn't been so hard.

Finally, as she was gathering all the grocery bags together, he spoke. "You got a Bible?"

She stilled and looked at him. "Yeah. Why?"

"Can I see it?"

She stuffed all the grocery sacks away and then retrieved her iPad, opened her Bible app, and handed it to Reece. He tapped in a few things and then flipped it around and handed it back to her.

He had highlighted two verses in 2 Corinthians chapter 5. Verse 17: *Therefore, if anyone is in Christ, the new creation has come: The old has gone, the new is here!* And verse 21: *God made him who had no sin to be sin for us, so that in him we might become the righteousness of God.*

Her shoulders sank. He wasn't going to listen to her. She started to put the tablet down. "Yes, Reece, I know—"

He took it back and glanced at it again. "Look at verse 19 too." He held it back out so she could see it.

"*God was reconciling the world to himself in Christ, not counting people's sins against them.*" He stepped closer and put the iPad on the counter behind her, gripping her shoulders again. He bent and peered into her face. "I'm a new creation in Christ—say it."

"Reece—"

He touched her mouth with the pad of his thumb. "Do you believe it? Are you a new creation?"

She sighed. "Yes."

"Do you think God is holding your past sins against you?"

She shook her head. "No, of course not."

His stance seemed to relax a little. "Then why are you holding them against yourself?"

"I'm not."

He tilted his head. "Aren't you? What makes you think you are not as good of a woman as Dakota or 'some other woman like her,' then?" He air quoted her own words back to her.

"It's not that I'm not as good as them, it's just..."

He pressed his lips together and waited, brows raised, but the look on his face said he'd be able to refute anything she came up with.

"I'm not as good as her *for you*." The words sounded lame even to her own ears.

He laughed outright and placed a hand on the counter on either side of her, leaning close and giving her a slow wink. "I think you're wrong. And I'm sure going to have a good time changing your mind."

Her stomach did a slow pirouette, and her legs were feeling about as useful as cooked noodles. "Reece..."

"Hmmm?" A soft smile tilted his lips.

He was entirely too close for comfort. "Can't you see your reputation might suffer if you date me?"

"Anybody who would look down on me for dating you is not a person whose opinion I'm going to care about."

She sighed. "Sure. You say that now, but what about years from now?"

"Years from now. I like the sound of that."

Despair coursed through her. "Reece..."

He held up a hand. "You are selling yourself and God's Word short. You are not the same woman you were. We've all made mistakes. Just some are more obvious than others. But Jesus' blood wipes away premarital sex just as easily as it does gossip or cussing. Now I want to hear you say two things."

Her heart started to beat in earnest. "Yes?"

"I'm a new creation in Christ."

Giddy. That's how she felt. When was the last time she could say she'd felt giddy? She wanted this. Oh, how she wanted this. Slowly, she repeated it. "I'm a new creation in Christ." It sounded so good, she said it again, and then just stood there reveling in the wonder of it. She closed her eyes, doing her best to see herself as God now saw her. Not as a rebellious, blackened sinner. But as a pure, washed child of God.

After a lengthy moment she realized the room had remained quiet for a long time. She peeked her eyes open to see what he was doing.

A grin had bloomed on his face, and moisture was shining in his eyes. He was studying every plane of her face, and palpable joy lit his own. "Yes. Yes, you are. And I'm so happy about that." He touched her cheek and swept his thumb over her cheekbone.

"You said two things?" She rolled her lips inward and pressed them together.

"I did." A gentle smile accompanied the words. But

there was a hint of promise there that started a little fire in her belly. "Say you'll have dinner with me Friday night?"

Giddy. Definitely giddy. She actually giggled.

Was she really letting him talk her into this?

Yes, she was. And quite willingly, at that.

But she couldn't resist a little teasing. "I'm not sure I can. I'm supposed to start work for this man sometime this week. He looks a lot like you, and I wouldn't want to have people thinking I was dating my boss."

He threw back his head on a quick bark of laughter. "You're fired. Now say you'll go on a date with me Friday night."

She widened her eyes. "But you can't fire me! Some guy just brought me a couple hundred dollars of groceries, and I won't ever be able to pay him back if you fire me!"

The look in his eyes changed from humor to something more serious and a lot more dangerous.

The little fire in her belly was threatening to become an all-out inferno.

"Oh, I'm sure if he thinks he needs to be repaid, he'll come up with some form of payment that should suffice." His gaze lingered on her lips as a hint of what he meant.

A curl of desire coursed through her.

She swallowed and gripped the counter tightly to keep herself from leaning forward and kissing him. That was something the old Marie would have done. "Thank you. For the groceries."

"My pleasure. I thought I was going to catch it from you there for a minute."

"You just might if you do something like it again."

He grinned. "Is that a promise?"

Anticipation zipped through her, but she wasn't ready to go there. Yet. "You also paid my co-pay at the hospital, didn't you?"

He straightened and deliberately looked around for a clock. "What time is it? I really better be going. I know you have to work in the morning." He snagged his hat, tipping it back onto his head.

She laughed. "Smooth. Very smooth. And not suspicious at all!"

He settled his hands on his hips and grinned down at her. "You haven't answered my question."

Slipping her phone from her back pocket, she gave it a quick glance, then held the face toward him. "Seven fifteen."

His boots scuffed against the linoleum as he tipped her a "be serious" look.

She tucked her lower lip between her teeth. Was that vulnerability she saw on his face? She certainly was feeling a good measure of it herself. She wanted to agree. She just didn't want to see him hurt. But either way, she would hurt him.

Finally she squeezed out the word that terrified her and filled her with elation all at the same time. "Yes."

Chapter 11

Reece growled and shoved his phone into his pocket before pulling his work gloves back on. Why couldn't Mom just leave well enough alone?

The past two days had dragged by. And nothing seemed to go easy. Dad was slipping further and further away and taking little pieces of Reece's heart every time he stepped in to see him. The riding mower broke down, and it had taken him the good part of this morning to get it running again. And last night there'd been a huge storm, so here he was, spending time he didn't have, getting the beach cleaned up because they had a slate of new guests arriving this afternoon.

And now Mom had just called to inform him she'd invited Dakota to dinner tonight, so he should be on time. Maybe if he hadn't told her he was going out with Marie tomorrow, she wouldn't still be pushing so hard with this Dakota thing. Dakota was one of the sweetest girls he knew, and he didn't want her getting hurt because Mom couldn't bring herself to accept reality.

He hucked another armload of driftwood onto the big pile he'd been building up and swiped a palm against the sweat starting to sting his eye.

"Need any help with that?"

Reece spun around. “Justus!” He strode toward the man who’d been more friend than boss to him for the past four years and wrapped him in a big bear hug. “What are you doing here, man?”

“Wow, you stink.” Justus teasingly shoved him away and took an exaggerated step backward.

Reece laughed. “Some guy I know used to say if you don’t stink when you get done with a job, you didn’t do it right.”

Justus laughed. “It’s good to see you.” His gaze turned serious, and he chewed the inside of his lip. “How are you holding up?”

Reece sighed and sank onto one of the larger pieces of driftwood, gesturing for Justus to join him. “It’s been a bit rough. Watching Dad slip away...trying to keep up a cheerful attitude when I’m in with him...my mom’s trying to put on a good face for everyone, and I know she’s got to be crumbling inside...she’s pushing me together with a girl I’m not interested in, and upset about a reconnection I’m trying to make with an old girlfriend I *am* interested in.”

Justus cocked him a hard look. “Is that the same girl you were running from when you first came to work for Deschutes Rejuvenation?”

“It is.”

“Reece...”

“Don’t worry. I’m not backsliding. She gave her life to the Lord, and...she’s pretty amazing.” He grinned at Justus, not caring if the man saw him for the lovesick sap he was.

Justus scooped up some sand and trickled the grains back and forth between his hands. “That’s good to hear. How are you holding up with your dad?”

A breath puffed out before he could stop it, and

Reece scrubbed at the back of his neck. "This is the hardest thing I've ever done. I keep hoping and praying to see improvement. And every day he gets a little bit weaker."

"I remember feeling just like that when I lost my dad. But I didn't have the Lord then. Just keep trusting and looking up. Remembering this world is not our home. We're all just passing through."

Reece swallowed. Nodded. Wished it was easier to believe.

Justus dusted off his hands and clapped Reece on one shoulder. "Come on. I'm here to help out for a couple of weeks. I had some vacation coming. So put me to work." He stood and pulled off his leather jacket and set to rolling up his sleeves.

Reece closed his eyes as a wave of thankfulness washed over him. It was just like Justus to jump in and offer to help where no one had asked him. And, honestly, Reece couldn't be more thankful for the help. There was so much to do around here. The more work he'd done, the more he'd noticed other things that had been let slip. Dad must have been slowing down quite a bit even before he took sick.

He stood and studied his friend. "You're going to spend your two weeks of vacation helping me with repairs?"

Justus folded his arms and tipped his chin to one side. "Just keep talking, and I'll book myself a ticket to Hawaii so fast you won't know what hit you."

Reece laughed. "You've had a long drive. Go rest. You can start helping me work tomorrow."

"Nah, man. I'm good."

"Where's your stuff?"

"I left it on the back of my bike, and unless you're

afraid someone's gonna steal it right out of your driveway, then it's fine. Now what are we doing here?"

Reece grinned and slapped him on the back. "Well, trust you to arrive when there's only half an hour left. We have to go in to dinner at six sharp, or risk The Wrath."

Justus lifted his palms. "You know it. I always have impeccable timing."

Reece pointed out the large rock down the shoreline that indicated the end of their portion of the beach, and both men set to work clearing debris again. And despite Justus's joking about Reece's scent, by the time the half hour was up, both men were soaked with sweat and needing a shower. But together they'd accomplished more than Reece could have done on his own in twice the time.

Reece held out his hand to Justus in thanks. "Come on, let's go catch a shower before dinner."

Dakota Trask swallowed her apprehension and checked her hair in the mirror one more time. Then she paused to give herself a firm look. "Remember his mother set this up and he's obviously interested in Marie. So don't make a fool of yourself. Just go and have fun and enjoy a meal cooked by someone other than you. And for heaven's sake"—she tapped a finger to her mirror nose—"try not to talk to yourself when anyone else is around." She rolled her eyes at her silliness, grabbed up her purse, the still-warm rolls, and her keys, and locked her apartment door behind her.

When she pulled into Serenity Shores, there was a motorbike—a huge red motorbike—sitting in the driveway. Her heart dropped. *Please, God...don't tell me Reece bought that thing*. She climbed out of the car and pulled the rolls she'd made from the passenger seat. One of the points on her red handkerchief-hem skirt was flipped up. She studied the bike as she bent down to smooth her skirt into place.

A BMW logo emblazoned the fuel tank. And plush leather seats stretched the length of the huge machine. She shuddered and averted her gaze, unwilling to take in any more details.

But it was too late to prevent the flashback to a dark rainy night, the contrasting feel of cool air against the backs of her hands and the warmth of Jason's leather jacket against her palms as she'd held tight to him. Their laughter as they sped along the coastal highway. Blinding headlights. Squealing breaks. Gouging gravel. Darkness and pain. So much pain.

She pushed away another shudder. It didn't matter if Reece was only interested in Marie. He was still her friend, and if he'd bought that thing, she was going to kill him. She pressed the doorbell.

Mrs. Cahill answered and waved her in. "You don't have to ring the bell, dear. You are welcome here anytime. You just come right in. Oh, and you brought rolls. Aren't you just a sweetheart." She grabbed the towel-wrapped basket from Dakota and shooed her toward the dining room. "Reece is already waiting in there. You just go on in, and I'll be right there." Reece's mom bustled off in the direction of the kitchen.

Dakota checked her reflection quickly in the entryway mirror, smoothing her hands over the black lace vest she'd paired with a white blouse and the gypsy skirt. She didn't know why she was so nervous about tonight except she planned to tell Reece she was sorry his mother kept trying to throw them together when he was obviously not interested, and she felt okay with that. It was bound to be a bit awkward, yet freeing, she hoped, too, to their friendship. She'd left her hair down and straight tonight because she'd been determined not to look like she was trying too hard.

"Get moving," she whispered to her reflection. Okay, fine. She looked good enough to tell a guy she didn't mind if he wanted to be with someone else. She poked her head into the dining room.

Reece was stretched into a chair. His chin rested in one hand, and he was staring off into nothingness. A big frown creased his forehead. Poor guy looked like the weight of the world was resting on him.

"Hey," she said softly.

"Dakota." He rose to his feet and smiled, but it appeared to take some effort.

Compassion pinched her chest. His dad must not be doing so good. She gave him a sisterly hug and then leaned back. "Your dad doing worse?"

Reece sighed. "He wasn't really lucid each time I checked on him today."

"I'm so sorry. I wish there was something I could do. Your dad is an amazing man."

"I know you do, and yeah, he is. It's...really hard to lose him. I know you understand."

Yes, she did. And on that note, it was time to address her concern. "Which reminds me...please tell me you didn't buy that red death trap sitting in your driveway!"

Reece chuckled. "No, that would be—"

"Mine."

Dakota spun toward the new masculine voice. The man was tall. Close-cropped blond hair that was a little mussed on top drew her attention to an angular jaw which hadn't seen a razor for a couple days at least, and a pair of piercing blue eyes that seemed to drill right through her. Broad shoulders stretched tight a blue T-shirt, and even from across the room she could tell the man was nothing but muscle—lots of muscle. Enough muscle to sear all the moisture right out of her mouth.

Holy hot hunks, Batman!

Hands clasped behind his back, he assessed her casually, and one blond brow quirked as he took in the jagged hem of her skirt. Humor touched the crinkles at the corners of his eyes.

Military probably, since he looked so comfortable standing that way. Former military? Or was he on leave? And was he laughing at her? Her eyes narrowed. It wasn't the first time her eccentric style had given someone cause for humor. But he didn't have to be so obvious in his disapproval. She lifted her chin and met him gaze for gaze to let him know his disapproval meant nothing to her.

In her peripheral vision, she saw Reece glance back and forth between them. He cleared his throat and broke the silence that had fallen. "Dakota, this is Justus, my former boss and good friend. Justus, this is my friend Dakota."

Justus stepped forward and held out one hand. "It's a pleasure to meet you."

His handshake was firm and warm and lingered a little longer than she'd anticipated, which sent a ripple of awareness through her that settled into tingles along the back of her neck. "You too." She tugged for the release of her hand and hoped the crazy mix of emotions she was feeling wasn't as obvious to everyone else in the room.

"Please, guys, have a seat. Mom should be right

here."

Reece motioned Dakota into a chair and Justus into the one directly across the table from her. She tucked her napkin into her lap and almost wished Justus had been seated next to her, because that way she wouldn't have to keep looking into those amazingly blue eyes that seemed able to see to the depths of her very soul.

Darlene bustled in with the bread rolls Dakota had brought and set them on the table. "There, Dakota, dear. I've fixed these rolls right up for you." They were now in a silver serving dish instead of the basket and kitchen towel Dakota had put them in before leaving her apartment.

Dakota pressed her lips together. Of course she should have thought about the presentation. She'd never seen anything but silver, crystal, and the very best of china on the Cahills' dining table.

Reece caught her attention and must have figured out what had happened, because he gave her a subtle shake of his head and a quick wink to tell her not to worry about it.

"Well, Reece, let's not keep our guests waiting. Say the prayer, would you?"

Everything was delicious and the meal progressed smoothly. After the meal was over and Mrs. Cahill stood to clear the table, Dakota offered to help, but the woman waved her off. "You and Reece take a walk along the beach. Justus will be glad to help me in the kitchen, won't you, dear?"

Justus's lips twitched, but he immediately schooled his features and stood to help. "Certainly."

Dakota checked the admiration that rose up inside her before it had time to grow too high. Any guy who drove a machine like the one parked in the driveway probably lived only to leap from one thrill to another.

Besides, this walk would give her just the time she'd hoped for with Reece. She slid her hand into the crook of Reece's arm. "Shall we, then?"

"Sure."

The view on the walk down the hill from the house couldn't be surpassed. The path was well maintained and bordered on the drop-off side by a split-rail fence. But it was the cloud-clothed sun, sinking low into the pastel horizon where ocean met sky, that made her catch her breath. "This place is so beautiful."

Reece nodded. He'd pulled away from her as soon as they'd left the house, which had made her feel a bit self-conscious. Touching was just what she did. It didn't mean she was attracted to him just because she'd touched him. But of course he couldn't really know that, could he?

"Listen, Reece. I wanted to talk to you—"

"Dakota, I'm very attracted to Marie."

She laughed. "Yes. I know. I was about to say I'm sorry your mother keeps trying to throw us together, and that I wish you and Marie only the best."

His cheeks puffed out, and he loosed a chuckle of relief. "I'm so glad to hear you say that. I didn't want to hurt your feelings." His eyes widened. "Not that I thought you were so into"—he waved a finger back and forth between them—"this."

Another bubble of laughter burst free. "I know what you mean. I've been debating all day how to approach this. I knew you were attracted to Marie, and wasn't quite sure how to tell you I'm totally fine with that without making it sound like you were a scourge."

"The next time my mother intrudes, feel free to tell her you are busy or just not interested in her scoundrel of a son." He winked.

"I'll do that." She turned toward the beach. "You must have been busy since the storm yesterday?"

He nodded. "Yeah, Justus helped me, or it wouldn't look nearly so good."

Justus. Her curiosity got the best of her. "You said he was your boss?"

"Yeah. I worked for a program called Deschutes Rejuvenation. He's the founder and owner. It's a program to help troubled youth—those in the court system—learn to deal with the junk life's handed them, and keeps some of them out of jail."

"Sounds interesting. What inspired him to start a business like that?"

"He was in the system himself. Served a few years. I think he had no one in his corner at the time, and he wants to be there for other kids struggling like he did."

So Justus had served time. Of course he had. Because every interesting man in her life was either already attracted to someone else, a felon, or...dead. Forcing herself back to the present, she rolled her neck to ease some tension. Yes, even if he *wasn't* a convict, his bike was an even bigger strike against him.

Despite the drawbacks, Dakota wanted to learn more but decided her questions had taken her far enough.

They stood studying the water together for a few more minutes, and then she excused herself and thanked Reece for his friendship, adding her best wishes for him and Marie to work things out. He walked her through the house to the front door. "Good night. And thanks again. Glad we had this talk."

She nodded and gave him a hug, then realized how he might take it and quick-stepped back. "Sorry. I'm just...touchy."

He laughed. "Good night, Dakota."

"Night." Relief was the only emotion she felt as she took the stairs off the front porch and headed for the driveway. "Thank You, Lord, that You helped me get through that! Onward to the man really meant for me, yes? Too bad Reece's sidekick, Mr. oh-so-hot-in-a-calendar-worthy-way, is obviously an irresponsible daredevil." She rounded the corner to find Justus eyeing her from where he leaned over the small trunk at the back of his bike.

Humor danced in his blue eyes.

An explosion of lava erupted in every pore of her face. Pretending great interest in finding her keys, she honed her focus into the bottom of her purse. How much had he heard? *Calendar worthy?* Had she really said that out loud? *Please, God, don't let him have heard.*

She should say something to him. But what did one say after a moment like that? When would she ever learn to quit talking to herself out loud?

She was nearly abreast of him. She couldn't just walk by without at least saying good-bye and "nice to meet you." *Be casual.* She froze and looked over, one hand still buried in the depths of her purse.

He still watched her. A quizzical amusement still danced in his eyes.

"It was nice to meet you, Justus."

He nodded, his lips twitching as though he might like to laugh out loud but was restraining himself. "Likewise."

"Good night."

"Here, let me get your door for you." He stepped around her and reached for the driver's side handle.

But she hadn't found her keys yet. Mostly because

her focus hadn't really been on keys but on the admittedly uberlicious man and his red death trap on wheels. She dug more frantically. "Let me just find my keys."

He waited patiently, his hand on her Honda's handle.

The key ring was huge with a large piece of marble in the shape of Africa dangling from it. How was it possible she couldn't find it? She grumbled a complaint under her breath and plunked the large silk bag on the hood of her car. She pulled out her wallet and a handful of receipts from the pharmacy where she'd picked up her malarial meds the other day, and plopped them in a heap. Next followed her water bottle, which started to roll as soon as she set it down and had her scrambling to catch it before it fell. That scattered the receipts, one of which caught in the breeze, scuttled across her hood, and wafted toward the lawn on a current of air.

Justus jogged after it.

Oh boy, she was a mess. Her bottle of Chloroquine was next. Hand sanitizer. Lotion. Tylenol. Small hairbrush. Compact. And then *triumph*! She pulled the huge wad of keys from a very bottom corner where they'd lodged under a couple bottles of fingernail polish. "Found them!" She held the set aloft.

One of his eyebrows quirked up. "You were having trouble finding *those*?"

Her face heated again. "Yes. I have a lot of junk in here."

He held out the receipt and eyed the assortment of things on the hood. "I can see that."

Hurriedly, she stuffed everything back into the depths of her purse and clicked the unlock button on the fob.

He beat her to the door and pulled it open for her. When was the last time a guy had held a door for her? Much less went out of his way to open one? "Thank you," she said as she sank into her seat and swept her skirt in after her.

He dipped his head. "It's the least I could do." He bent down and made sure he had eye contact before adding, "Especially since you called me calendar worthy."

She gasped and felt flames wicking up her cheeks.

He gave her a quick wink, tapped the roof a couple of times, and then pushed her door shut. As it clicked into place, it blocked out the sound of his soft chuckles.

Chapter 12

Nerves had Marie's hands trembling as she smoothed the fabric of her sapphire-blue sheath sundress for the umpteenth time. She angled this way and that in front of the mirror. Was it too much? He'd said Fisherman's Wharf, which was one of the nicest restaurants in town. She rolled her eyes at herself and turned away from the mirror, grabbing up her dangly cubic zirconium earrings. "Alyssa! Are you ready? We need to leave in just a couple minutes."

The bell rang at that precise moment.

She closed her eyes and inhaled slowly. Was she really going through with this? Was it selfishness on her part? Pressing a hand to her stomach, she hurried toward the door. The answers to those questions were yes and yes. But, so help her, she hadn't been able to bring herself to reverse her answer once she'd given it. And maybe it wouldn't be as bad as she feared. Maybe Reece was right. She believed the Truths Reece had read to her from the Bible that said she was a new creation. She just didn't have much faith in the kindness of other Christians to accept them.

She breezed past Alyssa in the living room and snapped her fingers. "Alyssa. TV off, sweetie. And grab your jacket."

She swung the door open.

Reece wore a dark brown suit with a forest-green necktie nestled against a lighter green shirt. The combo made his eyes even more vivid and attractive.

She swallowed.

His gaze waltzed over her, and a sparkle lit his features. "You look amazing."

"Thanks. You too." She cleared her throat and glanced over her shoulder. Alyssa still hadn't moved. "Come in. I just need to grab Alyssa. Taysia is going to meet us in the parking lot at Fisherman's Wharf to pick her up. I hope that's okay?"

"Of course."

She felt the soothing comfort of his presence at her back as she stepped over and turned off the TV.

"Mom! I'm *watching* that!"

Marie's eyebrows jumped up. "And I told you to turn it off and get your jacket. You get to go to Uncle Kylen and Aunt Taysia's tonight."

"I don't *want* to go!"

Teeth pressed together, Marie tossed Reece an apologetic look and moved to pull Alyssa's jacket from one of the pegs by the door. "I'm sorry. You don't have a choice tonight. I told you that."

"Mom!" Alyssa kicked out her feet and flopped back on the couch, stiff as a driftwood log.

Marie pinched the bridge of her nose. Alyssa had been grumpy and contentious since Marie had told her Dan wouldn't be coming back to see them anymore. She'd made sure to point out it was an issue between Dan and her and not any issue he had with Alyssa, but still the battles had raged all week.

Any moment the stiff-as-a-board pose was going to

morph into all-out kicking and screaming. Marie blinked hard. This was not the way she'd wanted to start her evening, nor the way she wanted Taysia and Kylen to have to spend theirs.

Reece stood quietly by the door, hands clasped behind his back in that casual pose of his, watching her, a soft expression on his face.

"I'm sorry," she mouthed.

He shook his head in a don't-worry-about-it manner and then pointed from himself to Alyssa with a raised brow. Asking her permission to step in.

Relief coursed through her and took some of the stiffness from her spine. She was most definitely willing to let someone else try to deal with the stubbornness of her tyke. Heaven knew nothing she'd tried all week had made any difference.

Reece strode over to the couch and stood over Alyssa with his arms folded. He gave her a stern look. "I believe your mother asked you to do something. Get up and go get your coat on. Now."

Alyssa looked shocked. She sat up, her little feet dangling over the edge of the couch. Then she bit her lip, a touch of embarrassment pinking her cheeks. But after only a moment, her little chin lifted and she fisted her hands. She assessed Reece as though sizing up just what consequences she might face if she rejected his order. "I. Don't. Want. To." Challenge glittered in her brown eyes.

Reece turned a questioning look on Marie. And she could tell he was asking if she was okay if he took it a step further.

She gave him a nod and a what-else-can-we-do sweep of her hands.

Quick as a blink, Reece picked Alyssa up, set her on

her feet, and squatted down to look directly into her face. "When you are told to do something, you do it, young lady. Get your coat on. I'm watching you on Monday, and there will be no TV when you're at my house that day because you didn't listen to your mom right away."

Alyssa's mouth fell open and big tears filled her eyes, but to Marie's surprise, she turned and buried her face against Reece's neck, blubbering into his shoulder.

Giving Marie a sardonic smile, Reece scooped Alyssa into his arms. "I'm sorry I'll have to do that. But it's important for you to learn to obey. Otherwise one day when your mom asks you to do something, if you don't do it right away, you could get hurt." He rubbed Alyssa's back and cupped the back of her dark little head, then winked at Marie over her shoulder.

"I'm sorry!" Alyssa sniffled into his shoulder. "Can I watch TV at your house, please?"

Reece wore such a look of compassion Marie felt tears prick her eyes. "Not on Monday, I'm sorry. But next time I hope that will be a reminder to you to listen."

"I will!" Alyssa wailed.

"That's my girl." Reece set her on her feet and squatted before her. Carefully he wiped away her tears, then chucked her under her chin. "Let's get your coat on, huh?"

Alyssa nodded and moved immediately to do so.

Marie held her pink Cinderella coat open and swung it around Alyssa's shoulders when she slipped her chubby arms into the sleeves.

Coat on, Alyssa turned and flung her arms around Marie's neck. "I'm sorry, Mama."

Marie closed her eyes and pressed a kiss to one soft cheek. "Thank you, baby. I love you. Let's go meet

Taysia, shall we?"

"Yes!" Alyssa was back to her bouncy, boisterous personality in the blink of an eye, and she bounded out the door ahead of them.

Marie reached out and squeezed Reece's hand when she passed him as he held the door for her. "Thanks for stepping in. She's been a bit of a bear for the past few days."

Reece's cheeks puffed out, and he leaned forward to whisper. "Let's just hope I can resist those big brown eyes when they beg me for a movie on Monday. This is going to be one of the hardest things I've ever done."

Marie chuckled and gave him a wink. "I totally know the feeling. One look from her and I'm a saucer of melted butter. Which is probably why things have gotten as bad as they did this week."

"Well, next time hopefully she'll remember the lesson."

Marie nodded. But what her mind fixated on was the fact that he planned to be around for a while.

Taysia was waiting for them in the Fisherman's Wharf parking lot and hustled Alyssa into her car with the promise of the latest Disney princess movie from Redbox.

Alyssa leapt for joy and clambered into the backseat to secure her seat belt around her booster. Taysia waggled her fingers and her eyebrows at Marie when Reece wasn't looking.

Marie wrinkled her nose and made a face, only to glance over and discover Reece's attention had returned to her and a huge grin had sprung up like a crooked sign.

She felt the heat that crashed over her.

His grin softened to a smile of appreciation. He

leaned close. "I'll have to make it a point to catch you doing things that embarrass you more often."

The heat burned hotter. "Why?"

One callused finger skimmed over the curve of her cheek. "Because this pink is absolutely enchanting."

The breeze picked up and whipped a strand of hair across her eyes. She glanced down, feeling the joy of being with this man puddle just under her heart. Her gaze couldn't stray from his for long. She sought him once more. "Being around you could be really good for a girl's ego. I better keep you close."

His eyebrows pumped twice, and he bent forward to whisper in her ear. "If that's all it takes, I promise to tell you how beautiful you are every day for the rest of your life."

With that he placed a hand to the small of her back and ushered her into the glass foyer of Fisherman's Wharf.

The maître d' led them to a table in a curtained alcove on the deck, and Reece held her chair while she sat. He slipped his hat off and hung it on the back of his chair.

The sun hung low on the horizon, splashing bright slashes of crimson across the smooth, rippling, inky surface of the Pacific. The breeze touched the torches at each corner of the deck and toyed with the orange flames. Marie watched the smoke dissipate into the gray-blue sky, feeling Reece studying her. She allowed her attention to fall on the man across the table, still hardly able to believe she was here across from him. She reassessed her decision to agree to this and found she was thankful for the curtained alcove, and it wasn't for the intimacy their little enclave afforded them, but because it was less likely Reece would be seen with her.

They could leave with his reputation still intact. A little stone of dread nestled deep inside her. Was this the way it would always be for her? Always wondering how his association with her might hurt him?

She forced her mind from the dark worries and sipped her ice water. "Thank you for bringing me here. It's beautiful."

He tipped a nod but assessed her thoughtfully. "Something is bothering you; what is it?"

She brushed away his question and flipped open her menu. "I'm fine. What are you ordering?"

She was thankful to see Reece slowly reach for his menu. At least he'd decided to drop the probing. He probably wouldn't like the direction her thoughts had wandered.

The numbers on the menu came into focus, and her eyebrows rose. She'd known from hearsay and from what she'd seen of the restaurant so far that this place was nice, but not *how* nice, apparently.

"Order anything you like."

He seemed attuned to her every thought. She swallowed and forced herself to skim the menu. She was going to quit worrying over every little thing and try to just enjoy this evening.

When the server returned and set a small loaf of sourdough bread with a portion cup of butter in the middle of the table, Marie's stomach rumbled in anticipation. Reece ordered a New York strip steak, medium well, a baked potato, and a Caesar salad. Marie chose the herb-roasted salmon with mashed potatoes and selected the salmon chowder soup for her first course. She closed her menu and refused to think about the fact that their meal tonight would have cost her a week of painting for Mr. Meyer, if she were responsible for paying.

Reece made small talk about his week as he sliced the bread and handed her a piece. She smoothed a little of the butter on the warm, soft interior, and her interest perked when he mentioned Dakota meeting his friend Justus.

Reece chuckled. "The tension was so thick we could almost have made a curtain out of it. And by the way, Dakota told me she wasn't interested in me, just so you know. But not before I told her I was interested in you." He watched her, apparently wanting to ascertain her reaction.

Marie wondered if Dakota had stated her lack of interest just to make him feel better after his declaration. Guilt once again reared its head.

Reece bit off a chunk and tipped her a look. "She wasn't just saying that because I told her I was interested in you."

Marie pressed her lips together and allowed herself to really look deep into his eyes for the first time that evening. How was it he could read her so well?

He dusted his fingers and swept his attention over the horizon. "So tell me what you've been up to for the past four years?"

Marie drew patterns in the moisture droplets on her water glass. "At work Taysia has trained me to teach several of the classes now. I really love that. Especially after...Alyssa. I don't know what I would have done without Taysia and the ladies at Mom's Gym during that whole time. God really used all of that in bringing me to Him." She shrugged. "Other than work, I'm just a mom."

The corner of his mouth twitched. "I don't think anyone is *just* a mom. And you've done an amazing job with Alyssa."

"Thank you. And what about you? Did you enjoy your time at Deschutes Rejuvenation?"

He nodded. "Very rewarding. Very draining. Very thrilling. And very discouraging. There were a lot of peaks and valleys to working there. I worry about my friend Justus because he puts everything into those boys, and I'm afraid he needs a break and isn't seeing it. I was really glad to see him even taking a couple weeks off. Surprised, really. Been praying for him a lot, lately."

That statement filled her with warmth. She loved how he cared for those around him. "And your dad? How is he?"

A weariness settled over his features, and she was sorry she'd brought it up. "I'm sorry. I shouldn't have asked."

"No. No. He's just...not doing so well. But we're thankful for every extra day we have."

Without thinking, Marie reached across the table and clasped his hand. "Your dad is a wonderful man. He has always made me feel special."

Reece's thumb stroked over her knuckles. "That's because we Cahill men know a good woman when we see one." He winked.

Marie laughed and was thankful for the arrival of the waiter with their food, which allowed her to extract her hand without awkwardness. Every moment with this man pushed her concerns for his reputation further from her mind. The level of her feelings for him scared her a little. She needed to keep things slow. Keep a level head on her shoulders.

The food was amazing. And after they'd finished their chocolate raspberry mousse and coffee, and Reece had paid, he stood and slanted her a question. "Want to take a walk on the beach?" He stretched a hand toward her, brows raised in question.

The sun had dipped below the horizon during the meal, and everything lay in the dusky gloam of the half-light between day and night.

"I would love to." She gave in to the temptation and took his hand, savoring the roughness of his palm against hers and the thickness of his fingers laced between her own. At the top of the stairs down to the beach, she pulled him to a stop to slip her high heels off.

"Reece Cahill?"

Marie felt a nervous quiver at the tone with which the feminine voice had said Reece's name. She glanced up. Capri and Paris Blackburn stood at the bottom of the steps in skimpy evening dresses. Their ever-in-the-sun tans glowed even in the twilight gloom.

"Ladies." Reece tipped his hat, but kept his hold on her hand. "How are you two this evening?"

The twins exchanged a glance. One of them shook out her long blonde hair and dropped her focus to their intertwined fingers as she replied, "Good. Not doing much. Just hanging out."

Marie had never been able to tell the twenty-year-old twins from the church apart. But she could certainly feel the malevolence being leveled her way from two very annoyed females.

"Well, we won't keep you. Enjoy the rest of your evening." Reece nudged Marie past them, and they strolled through the soft, loose sand to the firmer-packed damp area nearer the water. A few yards down the beach, Reece sat on a driftwood log and pulled off his dress shoes and socks and rolled his slacks up a couple turns. His hairy ankles stood at odds with the linen of his suit.

Marie chuckled and couldn't resist teasing him.

"Such a fashion statement, Mr. Cahill. I think it will be all the rage in the very near future."

He grinned and focused on her own bare feet peeking out from beneath the hem of her long sheath dress. "I guess we'll be starting this fashion together, then."

"Maybe." She was suddenly so full of emotion for this man it made her mouth dry, and she could literally feel her heart pounding against her sternum.

He swept off his hat and plopped it on her head, then tugged on the brim to pull her closer. While a twinkle still lingered in his gaze, the huskiness of his next words revealed a far more serious bent. "I've always wanted to start something with you, but it wasn't a fashion."

Desire to set aside her reservations whispered through her. Instead she forced herself to keep it light. "A business, maybe? Decorating! You build, I'll decorate."

The only reply he offered was a low rumble of acknowledgment in his chest as he stepped even closer and slipped one hand behind her back. He perused her face like the answers to all life's questions might be found there. His free hand tucked an errant curl behind her ear and fell to rest on her shoulder. His thumb stroked along the line of her jaw.

Marie felt a tremor rush through her. She needed to keep talking. This had become far too intimate far too quickly.

Her eyes darted to the fire pit just to their right. It was getting a bit chilly. Maybe she could distract him. "A fire, maybe?"

Humor returned to crinkle his crow's feet. "Oh yeah, starting a fire sounds good." But he didn't turn toward the fire pit.

The bottom dropped out of her stomach even as anticipation zipped up her spine. She licked her lips and then pressed them together. The strength of her desire for him terrified her. She'd given in to men she didn't feel a fraction of this emotion for, so what could these desires she was feeling entice her into doing?

He leaned closer, a request for permission lingering in his expression.

"Reece." She stopped him with a finger to his lips, which hovered just a breath from hers.

His nose brushed hers, and he pressed their foreheads together. "What?" No impatience touched his tone. Only a desire to hear her out.

She took a breath. "It terrifies me a little how much I feel for you. I'm afraid—I don't want—" She gave up and dropped her gaze to the gold eagle tie tack in the middle of his chest.

"Marie." He touched her chin and waited for her to meet his eyes. His words were barely a breath. "This feeling terrifies me a little too. But the very fact that you are questioning before you proceed is a sign your heart is changed. Feelings like this are a blessing from God. We just have to keep them in check until the right time." His thumb caressed the dip just below her lip. "This is different, isn't it? You feel something different—stronger than you've ever felt before?"

She swallowed. Oh yeah. He could say that again. She nodded, her eyes going a bit wide.

His fingers still lingered at her chin. "You don't have to kiss me if you don't want to."

"I want to." The whispered words popped out before she could think better of them.

Pleasure tipped up the edges of his lips just before

they claimed hers, soft and slow and sure. Gentle. Controlled. And so tender a sigh of total contentment escaped her. She allowed her hands to slide up his tie and around his neck, her fingers forking into the curls at the back of his head. His hat tumbled off behind her and landed with a squishy thud near their feet, but neither of them broke free.

Reece's fingers curled into her hair as his lips continued to claim hers. But he kept the kiss under rein.

A tremor of sheer desire coursed through her, and she wanted to step closer to him. To press herself into him so far he never got away from her. But that wasn't the kind of woman she wanted to be anymore. Not the kind of woman God wanted her to be. Not the kind of woman she *needed* to be anymore. God was her supply now. And He'd blessed her with this man who she felt so much for.

To keep herself from taking the step, she pulled her hands from behind him and gripped his wrists instead.

Reece pulled back a fraction, stroked one thumb over her mouth, and then leaned in again for one final kiss. After that he tucked her head to his chest. She felt a shuddery breath shake him. "You have no idea how long I've wanted to be able to do that."

Reveling in the sanctuary of his arms, and having no words to express her current feelings, Marie only rose on tiptoe and placed a quick kiss against his neck.

For a long moment they both stood watching the dark gray of the water lapping at the shore until a wave with more energy and reach than the others washed in and sloshed over their feet.

"Oh." Marie gasped at the unexpected chill and darted a few steps further from the water. The way she was feeling, it was probably good to put a little space between them, anyhow.

Reece bent to pick something out of the waves. "Now you've done it!" he teased, and turned to face her. "You dropped my hat in the water!"

She shrugged unrepentantly and gave him an innocent bat of her lashes. "I believe you knocked it off my head. So it's your own fault."

His eyebrows pumped. "Definitely. And I'd do it all again too."

At the hopeful note he'd purposely injected into the words, desire to be back in his arms lured her. But recognizing the danger of letting themselves get too caught up in this moment, she let a trickle of laughter loose instead, and took a purposeful step back. "In the olden days, cowboys used to let their horses drink out of their hats, so I think yours is going to be just fine. At least it doesn't have horse slobber on it." She grinned cheekily. "But maybe the slobber sort of worked in and acted as a softening agent." She scanned both directions of the beach. "I don't see a horse, but we might be able to find a sea lion."

He shook water from the hat and grinned at her with a retaliatory gleam in his gaze. "I'm lamenting the demise of my Stetson, and you are making fun of me? I do believe some retaliation is in order, ma'am." He drawled the words out long and slow.

She couldn't suppress a giggle of anticipation. Flirting unabashedly, she batted her eyelashes innocently. "Me? Make fun of you? Would I do something like that?"

Laughing, he strode toward her with a glint of promise in his eyes.

Marie snatched up her pumps from where she'd dropped them earlier, lifted the skirt of her dress, and turned and ran.

His bark of laughter preceded the crunch of his feet in the sand behind her.

Even though she exercised for a living and a glance tossed over her shoulder revealed Reece had paused to grab his boots and socks, it only took him fifty yards to catch her. Laughing, he swung her in a wide circle and then settled her into the crook of one arm. His breaths puffed hard as he grinned down into her face. "You are fast."

She was struggling for air in her own right, and not all of it was due to exertion. She poked him in the chest and puffed, "I let you catch me."

"Un-huh," he chuckled. "Sure."

Despite the fact that she had been joking, the truth of what she'd just said washed over Marie. She *had* let him catch her. From the moment she'd seen him in the grocery store and felt once more the powerful attraction they'd shared, she'd been caught in the current, and she hadn't even attempted to flee. She'd just floated along with it and it had brought her here, into the arms of the only man she'd ever really cared about.

She could hardly believe how blessed she felt right in that moment.

Reece's expression turned serious, and his gaze dipped to her mouth, but instead of leaning in for another kiss like she'd hoped he would, he let her go and stepped back. He slapped his hat against his thigh. "We should probably get going before..." He let the thought trail.

Warmth trickled through her. He was right. And she loved him all the more for it. Not many men in her life had cared for her enough to pull away and keep things slow. She nodded and tilted her head. "Thank you."

He took another step back. "Have mercy on a guy and don't look at him like that in the moonlight when he's trying to do the right thing, would you?"

A bubble of laughter escaped, but she obediently tilted her head forward and looked at the sand. "How's this?"

He chuckled. "Only a little better."

She grinned.

"Come on. How about we catch a movie?"

She nodded. "First let me make a stop in Fisherman's Wharf."

He nodded. "Yeah, me too."

As they made their way toward the restaurant, Reece slipped his fingers down her forearm and wove them between hers.

Marie sighed in contentment. She hadn't felt this wonderful for years. She certainly hadn't felt this much for a man, ever. She tightened her hand in his and tipped her head back. Above them the night sky looked like white glitter scattered over black velvet. *Thank You, Lord.* The short little prayer was thanks for so much. For the weather and the beauty. For the ability to breathe in the salty air. For the feel of still-warm sand between her toes. The feel of strong fingers cradling her own. The contentment in knowing she was loved and cared for. For the feeling that everything was going to be alright. For life, love, and happiness.

Reece released her hand as they separated in front of the bathroom doors, and Marie could have sworn she was walking on a cloud as she entered the ladies' room. The door slipped shut on silent hinges.

She just needed to do a little freshening up. Dust the sand off her feet. Slip her shoes back on.

She smiled softly at the ethereal glow in her eyes as

she met her gaze in the mirror, hardly able to believe how far she'd tumbled in such a short amount of time.

"What do you think he sees in her?"

Marie froze. The words had emerged from one of the stalls.

A second voice tittered. "Someone easy."

A stone of dread dropped into the pit of Marie's stomach. It was the twins; she'd recognize those sultry voices anywhere. A tremble started right under her heart.

The first one snorted. "She might be like that, but I don't think he is, is he?"

"What man isn't?"

"True."

"Besides, what else would he see in her? She's got a kid, for heaven's sake. And it's not like she's super pretty, or anything."

"I think she is. And it wasn't like she looked all Christian in that curve hugging dress she had on. Still, I'd think a guy like Reece would want someone with a little less...history than *her*."

Marie's eyes dropped closed. If there'd been any doubt who they were talking about, it was gone now. Her fists clenched and the tremble nearly took the strength from her legs.

The second twin hummed her agreement. "Yeah. I can hardly believe it. Maybe he doesn't know about her past?"

"Oh, he knows. He was there on Sunday when she was talking all about it. Standing out in the hallway like he didn't want her to see him, or something. Do you think she really meant all the stuff she said on Sunday?"

"He was? I didn't see him. I don't know. Can someone so far gone really change?"

Marie willed away the tears and quietly worked at slipping her shoes on. She needed to get out of here before they discovered she'd been listening to them. And Reece had been there? Marie pulled in a breath. He was so thoughtful. He'd probably known his presence there would make her doubly self-conscious.

"I don't know. But even if she has changed a little, you'd think a guy like him would want better for himself."

"Hah. You just wish he'd pick you!"

The first voice chuckled. "You got that right. He's so hot!"

One of them flushed, and Marie beat a hasty retreat. She nearly crashed into Reece as she rushed out the door.

"Whoa." He grabbed her shoulders. "Everything okay?"

She forced a smile. "Yes. Fine." If only she could tell him everything was as far from fine as could be. That their world had just come crashing down around them like she'd known it would. That he never should have asked her out, and she certainly shouldn't have agreed. It was her fault those girls were in there questioning his morality. Her fault they thought he only wanted one thing from her when he'd been nothing but a perfect gentleman all evening. Pain so sharp it threatened to steal her breath shot through her. She spun away from him before he could glimpse the tears that suddenly blurred her vision. "Ready?" She led the way out into the dark parking lot.

Chapter 13

A wave of suspicion washed over Reece as he glanced from Marie to the women's bathroom door and back. A frown furrowing his brow, he followed her out to the truck.

Something had definitely happened.

She was leaning against the side of the truck just in front of the passenger door, arms folded, eyes closed, and face tipped into the breeze. The wind caught her dress and swirled it around her ankles, but it was the stiffness in her jaw that set his heart to thumping in dread.

He tossed his hat onto the hood and leaned an arm on either side of her, purposely invading her space. "What happened?"

She sighed. "Reece..."

"Don't do this, Marie." He saw the glimmer of moisture on her lower lids.

Her fingers trembled when she laid them against his cheek. "I care about you so much. And I just...don't want your reputation to suffer because of me."

"It won't." How many times were they going to have to cover this?

"It *will*!" She stamped one foot and folded her arms

again. “I had such a great time tonight that I almost forgot. But you are too important to me, Reece. I can’t let you do this to yourself. People are going to talk—think false things about you—if you keep seeing me.”

“Let them talk. I won’t care.”

“But *I will.* We really can’t see any more of each other, Reece.”

“Marie.” He sighed in exasperation. What had happened in there? Had she overheard someone talking? He studied the bright glow of the glass-and-stone building. That had to be it. “Who did you hear talking in there? The twins?”

Her silence was all the confirmation he needed.

“Marie, those two have been gossips from the time they jabbered their first syllables. No one is going to pay any attention to them, and not everyone is going to be like them. And if you think I care a bit what they think about me, you’d be so far off the mark you’d be missing the target altogether.” He cupped her shoulders and tipped his head. Her skin was chilly beneath his. He rubbed warmth into her upper arms. “Come on, let’s get out of here.”

She wouldn’t look at him. “I think it would be best if we just got Alyssa and you took me home.”

Reece clenched his teeth. What he’d like to do would be to take the heads of a certain couple of twins and smack them together. Instead all he said was “Sure. That’s fine.” He leaned forward and placed a quick kiss to her temple, trying not to be too disheartened when she stiffened. He forced himself to take solace in the fact that she said the reason she was doing this was because she cared so much. “Come on.” He opened her door for her.

He spent the bulk of the ride praying. For what, he

didn't quite know. He felt unsure what else he could say to make her truly understand his lack of concern for any damage to his reputation that might arise from being with her.

Alyssa was sound asleep when they arrived back at her apartment, so he carried her up for Marie, like he'd done the other day. But all too soon he was once again standing at her front door fingering his hat as she waited for him to leave. He eyed her. She was looking everywhere but directly at him.

He made a hasty decision, tipped his hat onto his head, and took two swift strides to stop directly in front of her. He slid his hands around her waist.

"Reece," she protested, but she did look at him, and didn't try and pull away.

"I'm not going anywhere. I'm going to give you roses in public, and dedicate songs to you on the radio. I'm going to sneak up and hold your hand in the church foyer, and leave love notes on your car when you're at work and the grocery store. And everyone is going to think we're together anyhow, so you might as well not fight this. I love you, Marie. I think I have loved you since the first time you agreed to go out on a date with me. I had to move away because my heart was breaking a little more with every guy you chose who wasn't me. But look where God brought us? He brought you to Him. And He brought me home. Let's not throw this away." He held his breath.

She wanted to give in. He could see it. But in the end her stubbornness won out. "I just can't, Reece. *You* can't. Please, you just need to go."

"Okay." He returned to the door and settled his hand on the knob. She was about to learn she wasn't the only one who could be stubborn. "So Monday? What time do you need me to watch Alyssa?"

She blinked at his change of topic and stepped back, rubbing her bare arms. "Uh. Monday I work six to two."

"Perfect. So can we plan on working on the cabins starting about two thirty? I'll grab that paint you suggested for the bathrooms."

She hesitated but finally replied, "Yes, that should be fine."

He had a feeling the only thing that made her agree was the fact that she had no other options for Alyssa.

"Alright, see you then." He walked away, but shutting the door with things unresolved between them was one of the hardest things he'd ever done.

"Mommy!" Alyssa burst through the front doors and raced toward Marie Monday afternoon as she climbed from her car in the Serenity Shores driveway.

"Hi, baby." Marie squatted down and stretched her arms wide. "Did you have a good day?"

Alyssa nestled herself firmly against her and wrapped her with both arms and legs. "It was long! I got to play with Tawny all day, but Mr. Reece wouldn't let me watch any TV. I didn't think he meant it."

Marie bit back a smirk and glanced up to see Reece, one shoulder planted in the doorway, paint-splattered jeans and an old T-shirt doing nothing to disguise his good looks. Her heart stuttered, and she looked back at her daughter. "Well, guess what? We are staying a little longer because I'm going to be helping Mr. Reece do some decorating to the cabins."

"Longer!" Alyssa wailed. "Does that mean no TV *still*?"

"I'm afraid so. Bet you wish you would have just listened the other night, huh?" She set Alyssa down on the front stoop and, when Reece winked at her and gave her a supportive nod above Alyssa's head, did her best to ignore the flip her tummy gave.

Alyssa slunk over to Tawny, feet scuffing, and draped her arms around the dog. "I guess it's just you and me, Tawny," she proclaimed dramatically.

Marie spun away and pretended to be busy with her purse at the table to hide her laughter. Behind her Reece coughed, and she could tell he was fighting his humor, as well.

"Would you like anything to drink or eat before we head up to the cabins?"

Marie shook her head. "No, I'm fine."

"All right, then. Right this way, Superwoman!" Reece held one hand out toward the living room.

Alyssa sighed as though he might be ushering her to her death.

Marie hurried past him to lead the way.

Mr. Cahill was awake in his hospital bed. His eyes lit up when he saw the three of them.

"Well, hi there, stranger." Marie walked over and tweaked his toes. "How are you feeling today?"

Even though his eyes smiled, Dave sighed. "Ready to go home." He pointed to the ceiling.

Marie's heart turned heavy. She pressed her lips together.

"Not today, Dad." Reece gave the man a loving and gentle slug in one arm. "You just keep fighting, and we are all going to keep praying for healing."

Dave turned such a look of love on Reece that Marie felt the awe of it. The older man's hand trembled as he scrabbled it across the bed in search of Reece's.

Reece stepped closer and took Dave's hand firmly in his.

Finally gripping Reece's hand, Dave eased out a tremulous breath of satisfaction. "It is not our job to ask why, son, but to ask how we can bring God the glory through this situation."

Reece's face scrunched up in such pain, Marie's heart twinged. "I know, Pop. I'm trying. I really am. I'm also still praying."

"I couldn't be more proud of the man you've become." The older man's hand trembled as he patted Reece's.

"Thanks, Dad."

Dave nodded. "Now go on and have a good time with your two girls."

Reece cast her a quick look that contained so much promise it nearly took her breath away, then turned back to his father. "I plan to do that."

Guilt niggled at Marie as she trailed Reece and Alyssa up the path to the cabins. He already had a great deal of pain in his life, and she'd caused him more. It would have been a lot easier for him if she had stood her ground in the first place and not gone out with him to begin with. She'd better keep that in mind for the future. Because judging by the passion in his eyes when he'd leveled her with that look back there, he didn't plan to back off from what he'd said he was going to do the night before. Not even a little bit.

She was a touch nervous over what he might say once they were alone in the small space of the bathroom, with Alyssa engrossed at the kitchen table with a box of markers and a pad of drawing paper Reece had apparently bought for her, but Reece didn't say anything, only handed her a brush and set to work with the roller while she did the trim.

The soft blue she'd chosen for the colors of this cabin brought to mind the ocean on a bright sunny day. She envisioned the seashells she'd planned for a border, and a picture of a sailboat framed in white. A few white candles and white-and-navy accents would put some nice finishing touches on the place.

She set her brush on the lip of her can and reached to move the ladder a little further down the wall.

"Here, let me."

Reece reached around her with both arms, lifted the ladder, and shuffled them several steps in the right direction, then set it back on the floor.

Marie tried to ignore the ripple and play of muscles in his forearms, but it wasn't much use. For the heartbeat of one moment, she stood still between the arms he kept on the ladder; then she felt the warmth of his breath on her neck and heard him whisper her name.

She ducked under his arm and retrieved her can. "Thanks." She whisked past him and scooted up the ladder.

She heard a breath leave his lungs in a rush. "Well, I can see that some time and distance from last night haven't changed your mind. But I'm telling you, my mind hasn't been changed either. And until you can honestly tell me you don't care for me, I plan to make as big a fool of myself over you as I possibly can, Marie Sinclair, so you just be expecting that."

With that he clomped from the room.

Marie plunked her can down on the ladder and closed her eyes, feeling the tremor rushing through her. The man was determined to be a detriment to himself. But surely if she just held her ground, he would eventually get the message.

They painted without incident right up to the six o'clock hour and got one coat of paint on each of the three bathrooms. Reece had held his distance for the rest of the evening, but walked toward her wiping his hands on a rag as she gathered Alyssa and hurried her into her coat.

"Same time tomorrow?"

Marie shook her head. "Tuesdays I have a longer day at work because we offer some evening classes. And Wednesdays I take Alyssa to Daisies at church, and I go to Bible study. So tomorrow I won't be able to pick her up till eight, and Wednesday I'll want to swing by to pick her up at four, and we'll just head home to grab some dinner before church. Taysia gave me Thursday, Friday, and Saturday off, though. So I'll be able to work with you all day those days." She bit her lip, suddenly unsure. Was he expecting more from her? "I hope that will be okay with you?"

He nodded. "Sounds fine." He clasped his hands behind his back and studied her. "So tomorrow you have a twelve-hour day?"

She nodded and her eyes widened. "Which means you do too. I'm so sorry. I should have thought to ask you if that was going to be too much. If—"

"Marie." He cut her off. "It's fine. I was only thinking of you. That's a long time to be on your feet."

"Oh." She laid a hand on Alyssa's head. "I'll be fine, but Alyssa generally goes down about seven thirty."

He nodded. "Alright. We'll keep that in mind." He reached out and ruffled Alyssa's hair. "See you tomorrow, Superwoman. And guess what? You even get to pick out a movie to watch tomorrow afternoon."

Alyssa smiled and without hesitation shouted, "*Frozen*!"

Reece chuckled. "See you tomorrow. Thanks for having a good attitude today even though you weren't happy about not getting to watch TV."

Alyssa shrugged. "Mommy says sometimes we have to live with the 'sults of our choices."

Marie's eyebrows peaked. So the girl listened sometimes.

Reece squatted in front of her daughter and looked her right in the eyes. "That's true. But what we can never forget is that Jesus' sacrifice for us means we can be totally forgiven for our mistakes, too."

Even though the words were directed at her daughter, the quick dart of a glance he gave Marie as he returned to his feet let her know the words had mostly been directed her way.

Chapter 14

Tuesday afternoon Marie glanced at the clock as weariness settled over her. Three in the afternoon. She had an hour break before their series of evening classes started. But the bathroom in the locker room needed cleaning, and the garbages needed to be taken out, and since Taysia had a meeting with the accountant right now, it was up to her to get those done.

She pulled open the cleaning closet that stood right behind her desk and dragged the cleaning cart toward herself.

"Can I get that for you?"

She spun around at the sound of Reece's voice, her heart hammering in her throat. "What are you doing here?"

He held Alyssa by one hand and an iced coffee from Sherri's Java in the other.

He held the drink out to her. "Alyssa said you liked these."

Liked them. She could practically live on those things. Her stomach rumbled in anticipation. She hadn't had one in so long she really was surprised Alyssa even remembered she liked them. They didn't fit into her budget.

"Thank you." She took her first long sip and then closed her eyes, sighing in satisfaction. "Oh man. That is good."

A satisfied gleam lit his green gaze, and he dropped one lid in a quick wink. "And one more thing." He lowered his attention to her daughter, who still clung to his hand, her little arm disappearing nearly to her elbow behind his big palm. Marie realized for the first time that Alyssa had been strangely silent where usually she would have burst right in and wrapped Marie in a loving hug. Now she noticed that one of Alyssa's arms remained firmly behind her back, and there was a hint of mischief about her features.

She tilted her daughter a glance. "One more thing, huh?"

Alyssa gave a definitive nod. "Yep."

"Well..." She searched Reece's face. What was he up to? "Let's have it." Marie had to admit that her curiosity was getting the best of her.

"Close your eyes," Alyssa instructed.

Marie narrowed Reece another look.

He gave her a reassuring bob of his head.

"Alright." Marie closed her eyes and held out one hand, expecting something to be deposited there, but instead she heard some scuffling feet, felt a brush of air, and then heard a few scrapes near her desk. Alyssa giggled. Reece shushed her dramatically. Marie chuckled and sipped her delicious drink. She probably shouldn't be allowing him this moment. It was only going to soften her to him. And she must resist that.

"Okay! Open!" Alyssa proclaimed.

Marie did, and her eyes just kept on widening. A huge bouquet sat on the corner of the gym counter just above her desk. All of it wildflowers.

"You didn't have those flowers behind your back, missy!" Marie bent down to poke her conspirator daughter in her tummy.

Alyssa guffawed and wiggled away from her fingers. "We trickded you!"

"Yes, you did." Marie quirked a you-shouldn't-have brow at the handsome man standing before her.

He only folded his arms and leaned into his heels, pleasure and promise tugging up the corners of his lips.

Marie forced her attention back to the bouquet.

Hot pink wild peas. Dainty white daisies combined with a few yellow ones. Three large sunflowers. Several sprays of deep pink wild roses. And ferns—both maidenhair and sword fern varieties. The huge pink bow tied around the vase was covered with silver hearts.

Marie felt the heat that touched her cheeks.

Alyssa jumped up and down, clapping her hands. "She likes it! She likes it!"

She did like it. Way too much. "Reece—"

"Come on, Superwoman. Time to fly and let your mom get back to work." He snapped his fingers at Alyssa, and when she ran over to his side, he wrapped his hands around her little ribs and literally flew her to the door like a mini superhero, complete with sounds.

"Bye, Mommy!" Alyssa called, arms stretched wide like wings.

"Bye, baby," Marie called after them.

Reece didn't leave her with any parting word, but Marie still faced her tasks with renewed energy, much to her chagrin. How was she supposed to keep a man who did things like that at arm's length?

It wasn't until she arrived back at her desk to find Taysia standing next to the bouquet that she even noticed the card.

Taysia held it out with a bit of a guilty look. “Sorry, there was no name on the envelope, so I thought they were from Ky and read the card.” Her brows shot up. “Oh la la, girl. Do not let this man get away.”

Marie’s face heated, and she snatched the card from Taysia’s fingers, now worried what Reece might have said. But she offered Taysia a grin. “Guess this is payback for the times I used to read the cards on the ones Kylen sent you, huh?”

Taysia laughed and headed for her classroom. “Yeah, let’s call it that.” She tossed a wink over her shoulder.

Marie gasped. “You knew!”

Taysia’s cheeks pinked. “Well, I was honest that there was no name on the envelope, but the minute I saw your name at the top of the inside, I could have quit reading.” She glanced at her watch. “Oh, look at the time! Better get my room set up.”

Marie chuckled, knowing full well Taysia always set up her room for her next class at the end of her previous one. “Uh-huh. You just run like the chicken you are.”

Taysia made some clucking noises as she disappeared behind the door to her classroom.

Marie turned her focus to the contents of the card, her heart starting to beat as if she’d just finished teaching a class instead of being about to start.

“Marie, I’m always short on words when it comes to describing my feelings for you. But allow me to say this bouquet reminded me of you. Wildflowers can grow in the most uncanny of places. (Saw some wild peas growing right in the middle of a rock cliff the other day.) I know you didn’t have an easy childhood. And you let that push you into some mistakes. But we are in the now. You’re raising a wonderful daughter in circumstances that can’t be easy. And you are doing it with God's help. I'm blessed to know you. You're blooming from rock. Always, Reece."

Marie's legs collapsed out from under her, and it was a good thing her chair happened to be right behind her, or she would have ended up in a heap on the floor. "This is so unfair, Reece Cahill," she murmured.

The outer doors of the gym burst open, and a gaggle of women bustled in, all chatting and joking with one another.

"Oh, flowers," one of them catcalled.

"Who are those from?"

"Probably from Kylen for Taysia," another piped up.

"Actually..." Taysia sauntered their way and either ignored the fact that Marie was shaking her head, or didn't see it. "Those are from Reece Cahill to Marie. Aren't they beautiful?"

"Oh, honey"—one of the older mothers in the group flapped a hand at Marie—"we're so thrilled for you! Come here, doll!" The woman hustled around the desk and pulled Marie into her plump embrace, then pushed her into the crowd of women all waiting to hug and congratulate her.

No matter that Marie sputtered numerous protests that she and Reece weren't really together; the women all ignored her. Finally she gave up in exasperation and hollered it was time for classes and everyone better go to Taysia's today because she was going to make their muscles burn so bad they'd all be feeling it for weeks.

"Sure," one of the women in First Trimester Fitness, the class Marie was slated to teach next, complained to the rest, "make those of us in her class pay! Everyone leave her alone!"

The gaggle of women only chuckled and dispersed to their respective rooms still clucking like geese pecking at juicy morsels of corn.

Marie was thankful to see Riley Ross heading for her classroom. She'd been trying to talk the woman into leaving her abusive boyfriend and getting the help she needed. Had been inviting her to church for weeks. Maybe tonight would be the night she accepted the invitation. *Please, Lord, help me to reach her.* Marie sighed and headed for her classroom.

Every class for the rest of the evening followed the same pattern, and by the time the night came to an end, Marie was ready to strangle Taysia for her part each time in informing the women that Reece had sent her the flowers. But it wasn't until they were locking up the door and heading for their cars that it hit her. She froze in her tracks, turned on Taysia, and plunked her hands on her hips. "He enrolled you in his scheme, didn't he?" Her eyes widened. "And if he did, then you *knew* and didn't need to read the card at all!"

"No. No. No!" Taysia laughed. "There, I really am guiltless. But I did get this text from him right after I left so you could read that yummy card." She fished out her phone and opened a text, holding it out for Marie to read.

All the message said was "Tell everyone" with a wink after it.

Taysia tucked her phone away and gave an innocent shrug. "I'm always very obedient when I'm told to do something."

Marie growled her disgust. "Just see if I show up for work tomorrow, Mrs. Sumner."

Taysia only laughed and waggled her fingers. "Better go pick up your daughter from her very handsome babysitter. Don't be tempted to linger long, or anything. You have to be at work bright and early tomorrow."

Marie was still chuckling when she sank into the seat of her car and still in high spirits when she pulled in at Serenity Shores. She tipped her head against the headrest and wondered what the sense in fighting for the reputation of a man who didn't seem to care what others thought of him might be. She dredged up the conversation between the twins from the night before, reliving all the pain of it. The way it had made her feel to know they were saying all of that about him because of her. But then she reminded herself not one of the women from the gym today had been anything but super pleased about the fact that she and Reece might be together. She sighed. "Yeah, but those are my girls."

She propelled herself from the vehicle. She wasn't going to solve this dilemma after a twelve-hour workday.

Reece met her at the door with a steaming cup of tea that he held out to her.

For one tiny moment she wondered what it might be like for them if she just gave in. Would it lead to her coming home from work every night to that five o'clock shadow below green eyes that held the power to take out her knees? Or would he soon tire of her and realize his mistake?

She gave herself a little shake and inhaled the tangy steam. "Thank you. It smells wonderful."

"It's herbal. I wasn't sure if caffeine would keep you awake?"

She chuckled. "Most days I'm drinking caffeine right up till I brush my teeth and fall into bed, but this is lovely. Tastes great."

He nodded in the direction of the living room. "Alyssa insisted on sleeping on the couch in near Dad."

Marie moved past him, still cradling the warmth of the cup in her palms. If there was one thing she never tired of, it was watching her daughter sleep.

In the center of the room, in the hospital bed, the soft rattle of Mr. Cahill's breathing grated through the silence.

The couch where Alyssa slept lay beyond him, on the other side of the room. The floor-to-ceiling windows on the ocean side of the living room let in moonlight that spilled a blue glow over her daughter's slack features. Her bunny was hugged close with one arm, her tiny rosy mouth full and pouty, and her curls splayed in disarray around her head.

She felt Reece standing in the doorway, but stepped over to look out the windows instead. A full moon cast a swath of gossamer light over the flat gloss of the Pacific and etched the evergreen trees to the right of the yard a stark black against the deep blue of the sky. Far out on the water, a ship's lights cast golden reflections off the surface. Somewhere an owl hooted.

And behind her two beings breathed. One, a death rattle. The other, soft sibilances of new life.

Had Mr. Cahill's mother once stood over him and loved the sound of his soft breathing? Had she brushed back locks of his hair and dropped kisses on his forehead? And how long ago would that have been?

She turned to look at her daughter once more. Life was so short. What did the future hold for her? Marie felt nothing but gratitude that God had opened her eyes to the Truth. What would life have been like for her daughter if she had continued to reject God?

Her thoughts turned to Riley Ross. The woman had once again arrived for class with a large bruise on her shoulder. And she'd once again ignored Marie's gentle urgings to get herself out of her situation for the sake of her child, while she still could. What would life be like for that baby, if she could never reach that woman? She sighed.

Suddenly she realized Reece was by her side. He stood, hands clasped behind himself, watching her. "Everything alright?" he whispered.

She nodded. "Long day at work. A woman I'm trying to help..." She waved the explanation away. "She needs to leave a guy she's with, but she won't listen to me. I worry about her." She gestured from Alyssa to his dad and back. "Life's short. And I just..." She sighed. "I don't know. It's been a long day and I'm just tired."

Reece moved to stand behind her and set to gently massaging her shoulders.

"Mmmm..." She closed her eyes and huddled over the warmth of the steam still rising from her cup.

He bent forward, and she felt the brush of his lips against her head. "You are a wonderful, caring woman with lots of pearls in your life."

"Pearls?"

"I heard a man describe life that way. Each mistake we make is like a grain of sand that enters our life, but God can take each trouble and make a pearl out of it. We can later take the wisdom we learned while pearls were being made in our own lives and use them to help others."

"I like that," she mused. "I do have a lot of pearls."

He gently turned her toward him and pulled her close. "Yes, you do. And sometimes when others look at our pearls, all they can see is the sand that put them there."

Tears blurred her vision. How true that was. "I should get going. We'll have to be here again bright and early in the morning."

Reece stepped back, and if he felt disappointment,

he did a good job of disguising it. Sorrow pierced her. Was she being like Riley? Refusing to let go of things she needed to in order to move on with the life God wanted for her? But she wasn't doing this for herself. She was doing it for Reece. That made a difference, didn't it?

She shook her head. If people could read her crazy, mixed-up thoughts most days, they'd lock her in a loony bin for sure.

Reece lifted Alyssa from the couch and nodded to the opposite corner of the living room. "Her bag is over there."

"Okay, here's the keys to my car." She set her mug onto the tray on the coffee table and slipped the keys into his hand. "I'll just grab her bag and meet you out there."

Marie headed over and lifted the backpack, but Alyssa had not zipped it, and all the contents tumbled out as the front flap fell completely open. Marie grunted frustration and bent to stuff everything back inside. Zipping the bag, she slung it over one shoulder and turned to head outside.

Mrs. Cahill stood in the middle of the room behind her, arms folded.

Marie gasped and put one hand to her chest. "Sorry. You startled me!" Where had she been a moment ago when she and Reece were talking? As she took note of the decidedly unfriendly expression on the woman's face, she swallowed. "What's wrong? Did Alyssa—"

Darlene shot a huff of disgust through her nostrils that cut Marie off midsentence. "Alyssa was fine." She tossed a glance over her shoulder at the door Reece had disappeared through. "It's you I'm here to talk about." Her focus swung to the fore once more and pinned Marie like a bug to a scientist's display board. "You and my son."

"Reece and me?" The repetitive question squeaked on exit, making Marie feel even tinier. But she cleared her throat and lifted her chin. Still, she couldn't help but wonder what she might have done to displease the woman.

Darlene tilted her head, and one penciled eyebrow shot toward her hairline like a misbehaving bat. "Listen...I know you already know this, but Reece has been a good boy—a good man—all his life. I just don't want to see him throw all that hard work away."

Throw it away? On a woman like her, Darlene meant. Marie's heart sank. She'd known she felt that way. But until now she hadn't had any proof. It had all been guesses—pretty good guesses based on the woman's actions—but guesses nonetheless.

Of course, what mother would want her son to throw his life away on a woman who'd spent her early years sleeping with any man who would have her?

Marie didn't have one word of defense for herself.

Darlene shifted and dragged one toe along the meandering thread of mortar that held the slate floor together. "I know you are trying to get your life together, but if you care at all for Reece, please let him go."

Anger bubbled up like an underground lava flow that had finally found a means of escape. Why was it everyone seemed to think she had somehow set her claws into him? "Let him go?" Marie spread her hands. "I don't have any kind of hold on him. In fact, the very things you're saying are what I've also been saying to him. So trust me, Mrs. Cahill, you're not telling me anything I didn't already know." Marie brushed past her, battening down her anger as best she could. "If you'll excuse me, I'll see my way out."

Why was she so angry when Darlene was only telling her what she had already been telling herself? Marie loosed a vocal burst of anger that came out part hoarse whisper, part guttural grunt.

Reece had left the front door open for her, and Marie suddenly realized just how fast she was moving. She thrust her hands to the doorposts to stop herself before she burst out the door and Reece witnessed how angry she was. *Breathe. Just breathe.*

Reece tucked Alyssa into her car seat, made sure her little head was resting comfortably on her blanket, and then closed her door and hurried around to the driver's door to lean in and start the car. The late evening air was a little nippy, and he wanted to keep the inside warm.

He leaned against the car next to the driver's door and folded his arms, tipping his head back to study the patterns of the stars overhead. Far down the hill, the ocean's subtle *shush*ing played an undertone to the evening symphony all around him. Wind in the trees, crickets and frogs, the soft hoot of an owl, and somewhere a coyote baying at the moon.

He'd just realized it was taking Marie a bit longer to follow him out than anticipated, and started to wonder what the delay might be, when she strode around the corner of the house. One thumb hooked in the shoulder strap of Alyssa's little bag, she kept her gaze to the ground. But there was a tautness about her demeanor that made him stand upright. "Marie?"

She looked up. And he would have sworn the smile she pasted on was as fake as a three-dollar bill. "Thanks again for watching Alyssa." She made to brush past him. "I'll see you in the morning."

He scooted over a few inches so that when he leaned

against the car once more, he prevented her from opening the driver's door.

Releasing a little grunt, she tilted her face to the ground, but not before he caught the jut of her jaw. Still, somehow he knew the anger wasn't directed at him. He glanced back toward the house, a furrow forming on his brow. "What is it, Marie?"

Her teeth were still clenched crooked when she finally lifted her face. She rested one hand on his forearms, which were crossed over his chest. And just the gentle warmth of her fingers sent a surge to his pulse. "I'll be fine, Reece. It just really has been a long day."

Concern tugged at him. He wasn't sure she was giving him the whole story, but now might not be the best time to discuss it. Forcing himself away from her car, he turned and opened her door for her. "Do you need me to drive you home?"

She bent and tossed Alyssa's bag across to the passenger seat, and then touched his shoulder as she sank into the driver's seat. "No, thanks. I'll be fine."

But as he watched her pull out of the drive, Reece wondered if either of them would ever be fine again.

Chapter 15

Wednesday passed in a blur, and before Marie knew it, she'd dropped Alyssa off at her Daisies class and was sitting in the back row of the Wednesday night Bible study. She checked out the slides on the large TVs to either side of the sanctuary and noted the passage they would be in tonight, then called up the correct passage on her iPad and pushed out a slow breath.

Starting tomorrow she would be around Reece for three days in a row. She was all at once thrilled and terrified at the thought.

She turned her eyes to the round stained-glass window near the peak of the gable. *Lord, I just don't want to be the reason for anyone's life to be messed up. I've messed up my own life enough. So help me to know what to do. The last thing I want to do is hurt him. His mother certainly seems to think I'm not the right woman for him.*

She felt someone slip into the seat to her right.

Had Reece said he was coming? She hadn't been expecting him. She glanced over and blinked.

Riley looked at her hesitantly and then tucked a strand of her red-blonde hair behind her ear uncertainly. Her blue eyes held a bit of trepidation. "I hope this is okay?"

Joy trilled through Marie. "Okay?" She threw her arms around the woman. "It's fabulous! I'm so glad you came!"

Riley seemed to relax. "Oh, good. I wasn't sure if it was okay to just show up. I was so happy to see you the second I walked in." She gave a sheepish stretch of her lips.

Marie squeezed her hand. "We're just about to start, but can I get you some tea or coffee? There're cookies too."

Riley's brow furrowed. "Are we allowed to eat in here?"

"Yes." Marie stood. "Which do you prefer?"

Riley glanced around like she was realizing for the first time these were real down-to-earth people she sat among. "Coffee, I guess. One cream. No sugar. And yeah, I'll take a cookie." Her cheeks pinked, and she laid one hand over her rounding belly.

Marie patted her shoulder. "I'll be right back."

Marie grabbed herself a cup of coffee and a cookie also, so Riley wouldn't feel self-conscious, and then hurried back so she wouldn't be alone for too long. When she stepped through the sanctuary doors, it was to see Reece sitting in the space next to hers and a broad-shouldered blond man she didn't recognize sitting next to him. Reece was leaning forward with his elbows on his knees and hands clasped together, and chatting quietly with Riley.

Marie squeezed past him and his friend and handed Riley her cup and napkin with a cookie, then sank onto the bench. She glanced between the two of them. "I see you two have met?"

Reece shrugged one shoulder. "Actually I saw you get

up and walk away, so I figured I'd just keep your friend company while you were gone."

He sat back and gestured to his friend. "This is my former boss, Justus Teague. He had a couple of weeks' vacation coming to him and decided he had nothing better to do than help me with repairs at Serenity Shores," Reece teased, but there was appreciation in the tilt of his lips.

"Nice to meet you, Justus." Marie stretched a hand past Reece, and Justus shook it with a firm grasp.

"Likewise."

Marie then sat back and swept a gesture to Riley. "And this is my friend Riley. This is her first time here tonight, so thanks for keeping her company."

Reece stretched a hand in front of Marie to shake Riley's. "It's a pleasure to meet you. Sorry I didn't think to introduce myself sooner."

Marie went soft inside. He was so thoughtful to make Riley feel welcome and included.

Riley still had a bit of the deer-in-the-headlights look as she shook first Reece's hand and then Justus's. She deflected his concern with assurances all was fine. But then she turned to look at Marie. "The bouquet guy?"

Reece's warm chuckle accompanied the heat that flared through Marie's cheeks and the arching of Justus's brows.

Reece stretched one arm along the back of the pew behind Marie and held out a thumbs-up to Riley. "Yes, I am the bouquet guy. Those were nice, weren't they? A guy should get a lot of credit for bringing something like that to a woman's work, shouldn't he?"

Riley grinned, the first true happiness Marie had seen from her since she walked in. "Oh no you don't, Slick. I'm not going to gang up with you on Marie. If you can't win her on your own merit, then you don't deserve her."

Justus guffawed and slapped Reece on the back at that. "She's got your number."

Reece only laughed and squeezed Marie around the shoulders. "Wow, I'm going to have to find you some nicer friends." But there was no animosity in the words, and Riley's tinkling laughter proved she'd taken the teasing well.

"You better watch out for this guy, Marie."

"I know." Marie eyed Reece, feeling a warm contentment momentarily override her concern for his reputation. Would it be so bad to let this wonderful man fully into her life?

Movement across the room drew her attention to the Blackburn twins, who spoke low with a small group of women. Several of them kept casting not-so-subtle looks in her direction. One of the twins actually rolled her eyes at Marie, then shook her blonde hair over one shoulder and plopped down on a bench.

A cold chill stole Marie's contentment, and she leaned forward, hoping Reece would take the hint and remove his arm from behind her.

Slowly he did, as the study leader stepped into the podium. But when Reece leaned forward onto his elbows, a hard lump had formed in his jaw and his gaze was fixed in the direction of the Blackburn twins.

It was only a moment later that he leaned close and whispered, "I see the pearls, Marie. If others can only see the sand, it's their loss. Please don't make it mine."

Marie closed her eyes, willing away the agony washing through her. Why did this decision have to be so hard? Why did it bring Reece pain no matter which path she took?

Reece pulled his truck to a stop in the garage, yanked the keys from the ignition, and sank his head against the headrest as the electric door trundled its way closed. Why was it that church people could be some of the most uncaring, uncompassionate people on the planet?

Pain sliced into his palm, and he eased up on the strength with which he fisted the keys.

His feet felt heavy and weighted as he swung them to the cold cement and banged the truck door shut. A press of the fob chirped the locks into place, and he pushed wearily into the house.

The worst part was, it hadn't only been the Blackburn twins. Mom had been there too. In another part of the building with her own Bible study group, but at the end of the night when she'd walked by them as they were talking in the foyer, she had given Marie such a disdain-filled glower that he'd wanted to grab her and make her apologize right then and there.

Marie had stiffened noticeably, and been distant for the rest of what remained of the short evening.

Dakota arrived and Marie introduced her to Riley, and the three of them chatted, and since Justus excused himself soon after, Reece felt like a fourth leg on a three-legged stool. But he wanted one more chance to talk to Marie before the night ended.

After Dakota and Riley left, Marie bid him a rather frosty good evening, but not before she asked him once more not to make any more grand gestures.

"The flowers were great, Reece. So thank you. But it will just be better all around if you keep your distance. I don't want Alyssa getting hurt like she did when Dan and I broke things off." She'd trembled when she said it, and he knew the request had cost her.

Now as he plunked his keys onto the key rack, his teeth smacked together. He felt vacant. Like a treasure chest recently emptied. But he wasn't the kind of guy to force his attentions on a woman who kept insisting she didn't want them. So where was the line in this situation when he was fairly sure Marie enjoyed his company, but was trying to do what she thought was best for him? Maybe he needed food.

But Mom was in the kitchen cleaning the fridge out like a madwoman, and she was the last person he wanted to see at the moment. Milk, and Tupperwares of leftovers, and pickles and jams were all over the counters. He should have thought to hit up the burger drive-through on the way out from town. He turned to leave.

"You're making a fool of yourself over that girl."

He stilled and pinched the bridge of his nose, keeping his back to her so she wouldn't see the sheer anger pulsing through him at that moment. "No, Mom. But some people certainly are."

"Reece, honey. That's not fair. I only want you to be happy. And I don't think you're going to find it with a woman like her—"

"A woman like *her*?" He spun around so quickly his arm knocked one of the Tupperwares, and it scooted across the counter like a hockey puck. "A woman who works multiple jobs and still manages to keep her little girl happy and healthy? A woman who has a heart so tender for those who are where she's been that she goes out of her way to make them feel included and special? A woman who is *forgiven* by the grace of God? That kind of woman, Mom? Yeah, that would be terrible." He stalked down the hallway to his room, knowing he might have to apologize later, not necessarily for what he'd said, but the way he'd said it. Tonight he was too weary and disgusted to do so.

But as he sank onto his bed, a thought struck him so forcefully he shot back to his feet. He retraced his steps down the hall and slammed his palms on the island in the kitchen.

Mom jumped so hard she clipped her head on the handle of the freezer. "Ow! Reece, what has gotten into you?"

"What did you say to her last night?"

With a guilty look, Mom returned her rag to the shelf she'd been wiping down.

"You did say something to her, didn't you? After I took Alyssa out to her car?"

The only indication she'd heard him was the tightening of her shoulders.

"Unbelievable!"

Mom turned on him and shook her rag in his direction. "I was only trying to save you from yourself. It's obvious you aren't listening to any of my warnings where she's concerned. So it was time to step in and ask her to put you ahead of herself for a change."

"No, Mom. Stop!" Reece gripped the edges of the granite island countertop so forcefully it was a wonder the rock didn't disintegrate to dust in his hands. "This is about *you*! Not about me. I don't give a rip whether other people look down on me for being with her. But you certainly do. You didn't do that for me. You did it for you. Heaven help us if anything about the Cahills isn't exactly perfect, right? Last time I read my Bible, Jesus was more angry with religious self-righteous people than He was with truly repentant sinners." With that he spun on his heel and stormed back to his room. He snatched off his boots and jeans and traded them for shorts and running shoes. He needed to run off some steam, and quickly, before he put his fist through something.

Thursday morning Marie arrived at Serenity Shores in grubby jeans and a paint-splattered T-shirt. The first thing they were going to do this morning was comb the beach for unbroken shells, sand dollars, and usable pieces of driftwood.

Reece's friend, Justus, manned a weed eater along the edges of the driveway and paused long enough to raise a hand in greeting.

Alyssa bounced at her side as they waited for someone to answer the door.

Mrs. Cahill was the one who pulled the door open. Her gaze slipped over Marie from the messy ponytail she'd gathered at the top of her head to the toes of her paint-stained shoes. Marie had expected to see the normal disapproval but today there was something different in Darlene's assessment. Almost sorrow. Almost an apology. Almost regret. But all of them not quite tangible. Darlene's focus swerved to Alyssa. Marie was gratified to see a total softening in the woman's expression when it came to her daughter.

Darlene stepped back. "Please come in." She pointed at Marie. "Reece asked me to just have you come on up to the cabins. And what about you, little miss?" Darlene bent down to peer right into Alyssa's big brown eyes. "Would you like to stay here and help me make cookies in the kitchen?"

"Can I?" Excitement practically had Alyssa wiggling like a puppy.

Marie felt hesitant. She laid a hand on Alyssa's head to still her before she knocked something expensive over. "I don't want her to be a bother."

Darlene waved her off. "No bother at all. And I'll bring her up when we're done so I can see the progress up there. To hear Reece go on, you've done wonders for the places." Darlene's mouth twisted to one side, but a bit of kindness settled around her eyes. "Can I get you some coffee before you go up?"

"Thanks, but I had some before we left the house. I'm good." She bent and kissed Alyssa on one cheek. "Be a good helper, okay? I'll see you in a little bit?"

"Bye, Mama!" Alyssa threw herself so forcefully against Darlene's legs to hug her knees and look up at her that the woman gave a startled chirp and flailed her arms to catch her balance. Alyssa didn't seem to notice. "What kind of cookies are we making?"

"I'm so sorry," Marie blurted. "Are you alright?"

Darlene batted away her concern. "She's just a little girl full of life. It's good for me to be jolted once in a while." The smile she offered was the first genuine smile lacking disapproval Marie had ever received from the woman. "Go on. We'll be fine. And"—she turned her attention back to the human octopus wrapped around her legs—"what do you say to chocolate chip?"

"My favorites!" Alyssa spun a little jig.

Marie was still chuckling as she made her way through the living room toward the back patio.

She noticed Dave Cahill watching her progress, the twinkle in his eyes almost disguising the parchment-thin dry skin which sagged along his jawline. She paused. "Hi there. You look a little better today."

He nodded and waved her closer. "So glad to see you! Is that young one of yours here?"

Marie nodded. "In the kitchen making cookies with Darlene. If you're good, they might even bring you one later."

He smiled. "Chocolate chip, I hope?"

Marie blinked hard to keep moisture from her eyes. How many more days would he be able to enjoy such earthly delicacies? Darlene had obviously been thinking of Dave when she'd made that suggestion. Marie dipped her head to affirm Dave's hopes.

He sighed. "My Darlene, she loves me too well." He gestured Marie closer and clasped her hand. "We've had a good life, she and I. Humor an old man who sees much in the face of his son. He's carried a weight the past few days that goes beyond what he's feeling about my situation." Faded green eyes seemed to search the very depths of her soul as his fingers tightened around hers. "Don't let fear of pain keep you from enjoying the happiness life can offer."

He continued to probe her with such a searching look Marie felt it to her toes.

She shook her head. "I'm not afraid of pain." At least not her own.

The older man's countenance brightened. "Good. That's good. My Reece is a good man."

She swallowed. "Yes. He is." He deserved to hear the truth before he got his hopes up. And she certainly wasn't going to lie to a dying man, so she shook her head. "I'm afraid it's a bit complicated. I'm just not sure I'm the right woman for Reece, Mr. Cahill."

He started to say something but was seized by a fit of coughing. He pointed at the cup of water with the straw on the table by his bed.

Marie picked it up, helped him with his oxygen mask, and held the straw so he could sip.

Dave patted her hand and sank back against his pillow, spent.

Marie set the cup down and helped him adjust his mask once more. “I should let you rest.”

Dave clutched for her before she could leave. He wheezed in a breath as he studied her face, then tightened his grip around her fingers softly. “Don’t ever let anyone make you feel like God’s grace is too cheap to cover your sins.”

Tears welled in Marie’s eyes before she could stop them. That was exactly how she felt sometimes.

Movement drew her attention across the room. Darlene must have heard Dave coughing and come to check on him, but now she stood in the doorway with one hand covering her mouth, a look of sheer horror on her face.

Startled, Marie stood and glanced around. Seeing nothing out of the ordinary, she turned back to the woman. “Is everything okay?”

Darlene gave a jerky nod. “Yes. Yes. Fine. Everything’s fine. Thanks for—” She swept a motion toward Dave and then tossed a glance over her shoulder. “I’d best check on our little chef.” With that Darlene rushed from the room.

Marie shook off her curiosity over the incident and turned back to Dave. She leaned forward and pressed a kiss to his forehead. “Thank you for the reminder.”

Dave patted her hand again even as his eyes slipped closed. His breaths still came even and slow, so she slipped her hand from his and made her way up to the cabins.

Chapter 16

Dave's words echoed in her mind on the way up the path. Conviction washed over her. That really was what she'd done. Let people make her feel like her sins were too big for God to handle. Like she'd fallen too far to ever measure up against other children of God. When in reality even one little misstep from the line of God's law removed people exactly the same distance from salvation as those who ran and leapt as far into sin as they could sink both feet. It was the distance of a canyon. A canyon that had already been spanned by Jesus' death on the cross, if only people would put their faith in Him and walk across.

Marie paused halfway up the bluff. She glanced at the sky. The only thing marring the turquoise-blue expanse was one fluffy white cloud. *You can take care of Reece's reputation as well as my own, can't You, Lord? I'm a new creation. Help my unbelief, would You? And if there's a possibility for a future with Reece...*

She let the prayer trail away because just the mention of the possibility set her heart to beating so hard she could hear it in her ears.

That giddy, girl-on-a-first-date feeling was back. She would talk to Reece. Mention what his dad had said, and let him know if he wasn't opposed, she'd be happy to see where this thing between them went.

But when she reached the cabins, Reece was quiet and withdrawn, barely saying two words of greeting before he left her to finish up in cabin one while he went to work on cabin three. His father's failing health had to be weighing on him, and she knew she'd hurt him multiple times over the past few days, but she'd hoped to catch a bit of the guy who'd brought wildflowers to her desk at work and then made sure Taysia told everyone they were from him.

About two o'clock that afternoon, he stalked into the kitchen she was working on, grabbed up his truck keys, and swung them around one finger. They slapped repeatedly into his palm as he approached the area where she was putting the finishing touches on the second coat of paint. "I'm going to run to the hardware store and get those flower planters you wanted, and order up the sod we'll need delivered for the lawns outside. Anything else you can think of that we need?"

Marie pressed her lips together. From his all-business tone, now was not the time to discuss her change of heart. But there would be time. She just had to be patient. For now, there were a couple of things she'd wanted to discuss with him about the cabins.

She squinted him an I-don't-know-if-this-is-too-much look. "Could you check on the price of some freestanding fireplaces? I was thinking that on cooler nights, it might be nice for the guests to have those out on the stone patios."

He nodded. "Anything else?"

Marie eyed the light switch she'd been contemplating moments earlier. "Maybe you could bring back a couple samples of faceplate styles?" She tapped the switch. "It would be good to fancy these up a bit."

Reece rubbed his cheek against one shoulder. "Why don't you just come with me? Then you can choose the fireplaces too."

"Alyssa—"

He cut her off. "Mom won't mind watching her. Or we could just bring her with us."

Marie's heart nearly tripped over itself. Maybe this was the opportunity she'd been waiting for all day. "Okay." She tilted a nod toward her rapidly drying paint. "I need five minutes."

Reece dipped his chin in agreement and strode from the room.

A sigh escaped. "Ir-ri-ta-ble."

"What was that?" He poked his head back through the door.

"Nothing."

He grunted and left the room again. This time she held her breath until she heard the click of the front door shutting.

Darlene said she'd be happy to watch Alyssa, so Reece and Marie rode alone toward the home-and-garden store. In silence.

Reece finally huffed a huge breath and reached for her hand. "I have been irritable. I'm sorry."

Marie cringed guiltily. "I shouldn't have said that."

"No. Really. It's true. I'm not really upset with you, though; it's just, everything that's going on has got me down." He paused for a beat. Then squeezed her hand. "Well, that's not really true. I am upset with you a bit. But I want you to know I've decided to give you the space you're asking for. I really have no hard feelings. And to prove it..." He reached over and tuned the radio to a soft rock station.

Marie frowned, missing the way his fingers had curled around hers already. "I'm a bit lost, Reece."

"Just listen."

The current song ended, and by the time the set of commercials finished, Marie felt like a panic attack might be coming on. *I've decided to give you the space you're asking for.* When the DJ's voice came back on, Marie held her breath so as not to miss a single word.

"This next song goes out to Marie from Reece. Reece says, 'Marie, this will always be true of me no matter what the future brings us.' Aw!" The DJ sniffed dramatically. "That gives me goose bumps, folks! The song is *I Will Always Love You* by Whitney Houston."

The lilting strains of the first notes of music filled the cab of the truck, and Marie swallowed down her dread as she darted Reece a look.

A muscle bunched in his jaw, and he turned his face toward the panoramic view of the ocean out his window for a moment before resuming his vigilant driving.

The whole time she listened, Marie's pulse grew faster and faster. Had she ever really listened to this song before? It was about breaking up. Wishing the other person well. And moving on with life.

He was breaking things off before they even got started. Her eyes dropped closed. It was her own fault. She was the one who had set this into motion! "Reece—"

He held up a hand. "I know I've been pushing you, Marie. And that's not what I want you to feel from me. So if you aren't ready, then yeah, it's probably best we don't see any more of each other right now. In a dating capacity, I mean."

She swallowed. Was it really her feelings he was considering? Or was he just trying to ease her into his decision to see no more of her? She fisted her hands in her lap and nipped the inside of her lip between her teeth. *Confusion, thy name is Reece Cahill!* She should just tell him what his dad had reminded her of and confess she'd be flattered if he still wanted to see her. But what if he had finally come around to realizing he didn't want to have a woman like her in his life? Then her change of heart would just really muddle things up.

She tipped her head back against the seat and let her vision blur against the thickly forested hillside which rose to the east. Wide, flat ocean on one side. Steep, wooded hills on the other.

The landscape was so juxtaposed. Just like her and Reece.

For the rest of Thursday and all day Friday, Marie held her silence. She was tired of swinging on an emotional pendulum and wanted to make sure she knew her own mind before she confessed to him her change of heart. She also wanted to make sure she'd really had a change of heart and do some praying about the decision.

She still couldn't help but feel allowing him to date her was a bit of a selfish decision on her part, but at the same time that feeling was being washed away as she considered the concept of grace—an undeserved gift. There was no way to earn God's grace, and that was what she'd been trying to do. She'd felt she needed to be and do and perform better—even to *have been*, and *have done*, and *have performed* better in the *past*—in order to make herself worthy of God's forgiveness when all along He simply wanted to provide it free and clear. And if others couldn't see that, see the pearls God had built up in her life with His grace, then hard as it might be, she really wanted to let concern for their feelings go.

So she'd determined when she woke this morning that this would be the day. The day she laid her heart bare before Reece Cahill and let him determine her fate. Still, now pulling to a stop in the Serenity Shores driveway, she swallowed hard. Her hands trembled as she pushed herself out of the vehicle and forced her feet to move to the door.

Kylen and Taysia had been headed to the beach with Taysia's father and his wife today. And Taysia had insisted Alyssa would have more fun with them at the beach than she would sitting around waiting for Marie all day. Marie knew she was right, so had agreed to let them take Alyssa with them.

Now, as she pressed the doorbell, she regretted her decision. Darlene was always a little softer toward her when she had Alyssa with her.

Footsteps sounded inside, and there was a flash of movement through one of the full-length sidelights, and then the lock clicked open and Mrs. Cahill pulled back the door. Her lips pressed together in a thin line, and her eyes were red and puffy, her cheeks blotchy.

Oh no...

A small sob escaped the woman. "I'm sorry. This is not a good time. You'll need to come back later." She started to shut the door.

"Mom. I've got this. I'll be right back in."

Darlene lifted a hanky to dab the corner of one eye as she turned away without another word.

Reece stepped out onto the landing, pulled the door almost shut, and then shoved his hands deep into his front pockets and hunched his shoulders. He didn't look at her, but stared blankly across the lawn at nothing in particular. He looked worn, and thin, and ragged. His curls protruded from his head at several angles, as though he'd been clutching handfuls of his hair for long periods of time.

It had to be his dad. Forget what she'd come to say. She felt tears sting her eyes. Her heart broke at the thought of losing Dave. If she was hurting this much, how much more were they?

Marie reached out and stroked his arm. "Reece. I'm so sorry."

He blinked and focused on her, but he didn't seem to really see her. His eyes were vacant. "He seemed to be doing a little better yesterday. But then he really started struggling to breathe late last night. He...passed just a few minutes ago. The hospice nurse is on the way now to...pronounce the..." He let the sentence trail. His expression crumpled and he pressed his lips tight.

"I'm so sorry." Marie pulled Reece into a comforting embrace. Seeing him in so much pain made her chest tight and heavy. She wanted to ease his heartache. She'd take it all on herself if that were possible.

His arms came around her slowly, and he slumped against her, resting his forehead onto her shoulder. His torso shook as silent sobs racked through his body.

"I'm so sorry." She simply held him, one arm holding his head into her shoulder, unsure what other comfort to offer.

Her own tears spilled over and coursed down her cheeks to trickle, salty and warm, to the corner of her mouth.

Dave had been like a father to her when she'd dated Reece all those years ago. And, if she were to admit it, a better father than her own. She glanced toward the sky, imagining Dave free of his pain, free to breathe on his own, free from the physical limitations of his body, maybe embracing Jesus and laughing over how good it was to finally meet Him face to face.

After several minutes, Reece pulled back. He used his fingers and thumb to give a quick swipe to his eyes, and then settled his hands on either side of her neck. He took in her tears and cocked his head as he reached out with his thumbs and smoothed them away. "He's in a better place. We have to remember that. Much as I'm going to miss him, I wouldn't wish him back."

Marie nodded. "I know."

He leaned forward and rested his chin against his arm, staring out over the front lawn. "I'm sorry. I forgot you were coming today. I should have called and told you to stay home."

"It's totally fine. Don't worry about it. I would have wanted to come anyway."

He straightened and squeezed the muscles at the back of his neck and roughed a hand through his hair as he offered an apologetic look. "We're going to have to put off working on the cabins for a while."

"Of course. No problem. You and your mom take all the time you need, Reece. I'm so sorry." She felt like a sad song set on auto replay, but she couldn't think of anything else to say.

A gray-haired woman in a straight black skirt and sensible black leather flats came around the corner and stepped up onto the porch.

The hospice nurse.

She held a briefcase and wore a look of sincere apology in her expression.

Reece's shoulders slumped. "I'll take you inside in just a second." His focus returned to Marie. "I know you need the money; I think we can—"

Marie stepped forward and laid a hand on his arm to

silence him. “It’s fine. Really. Please don’t worry about me. Everything’s fine. I’ll head home, and you call me if you need anything, okay?”

“Actually, dear”—the hospice nurse stepped forward—“if you don’t mind, I’m betting Reece and his mother haven’t eaten for hours. Would you mind coming in and making a light breakfast for them while we get some paperwork filled out and other matters settled?”

Marie didn’t mind, but she looked to Reece for permission. He scrubbed his hand through his hair again, looking a little lost. “Yeah, I don’t remember the last time we ate.”

The nurse quirked an eyebrow at her to ask if she could stay, and Marie nodded. “Sure. I’d be happy to help.”

“Good. Reece, come on. Let’s go see your dad, honey.”

Reece led the woman toward the living room, and Marie made her way to the kitchen and set her purse on the counter next to the refrigerator. A hunt through the fridge revealed several vegetables and plenty of eggs, and there was a block of Gouda cheese in one of the drawers. It didn’t take her long to chop and sauté the vegetables in a skillet and then pour the eggs over it all. She let the eggs cook and then sprinkled some grated Gouda over the top and pulled the toast from the toaster. She found softened butter and some jam and put it all on the table. But the men from the mortuary arrived just as she started toward the living room. She diverted to the door and let them in, then led them to the living room.

Her heart went out to Reece and Darlene. It was going to be a long day for them both.

Tuesday, the day of the funeral, dawned sunny and bright. And Marie couldn't help but be glad about that. It was almost like Dave had asked God for a special blessing just for them on this day.

She dressed Alyssa and explained how she needed to be very quiet and thoughtful during the funeral because everyone was going to be missing Mr. Cahill so strongly.

"Can I bring my drawing pad Mr. Reece got me?"

"Yes, that will be fine." Marie slid the brush through Alyssa's last tangle. "There. Grab your stuff and let's go."

Marie had been to several funerals, all of them solemn and sorrowful. But at Dave's the focus was more on a celebration of his life than on the despair over the Cahills' loss. There was a slide show that started showing old black-and-white images of when he was just a baby and carried through his years of military service on through the early days of Serenity Shores and up to just a few days before he passed away. Shots of birthdays, and home movies of him cheering for Reece at Little League games. Anniversaries and Christmases. Each glimpse into his life showing a man who put God first in everything he did, till Marie's tears were more of joy for a life well lived than sorrow for what the world had lost.

The procession of cars to the cemetery was long, proof the man had meant something to many in Marinville and other towns nearby. The service there was short, though, and it wasn't long before Marie found herself standing before Reece and his mother.

She couldn't have been more surprised when Mrs. Cahill pulled her into an embrace, especially since it seemed genuine and Reece was engaged in a conversation with his friend Justus.

The woman set her back to arm's length. "I haven't been very kind. Dave's words to you really convicted me, but with all that's been going on, I haven't found the time to talk to you."

Marie's mouth dropped open, but she couldn't seem to find any words. Was she only saying this because Marie and Reece weren't seeing each other right now?

Darlene's face scrunched, and she dabbed at the tears flowing freely. "He was a good man. Could always see the good in people. Please forgive me."

"I—yes, of course." Marie pulled the woman into a hug of her own, closing her eyes in thankfulness. She didn't care exactly why she was apologizing; it just felt good to hear it.

Reece was still busy talking with others, so Marie took Alyssa's hand and stepped off to one side to wait to offer him another round of condolences.

She was determined to wait to tell him about her change of heart also. He didn't need any more emotional turmoil tossed at him right now. A gap presented itself, and she and Alyssa stepped in to fill it.

Reece's gaze softened as it landed on them. "Hi," he said softly.

Marie released Alyssa's hand and stepped forward to pull him into an embrace. "It was a beautiful service. It was wonderful to see all the highlights of your dad's life."

Alyssa tugged on Reece's hand and Marie stepped back, wishing she could take all his pain and yet realizing the pain was a sign of a man loved well.

Reece squatted down and peered into Alyssa's face. "Hey there, Superwoman."

Alyssa threw her arms around his neck. "I've missded you."

Reece blinked hard. "I've missed you too."

Marie hadn't been taking Alyssa to his place since his father had passed. Alyssa had done tolerably well keeping herself entertained at Mom's Gym, during the times Marie had to teach classes, and, thanks to her drawing tablet, kept mostly out of Marie's hair during the times she'd been behind the desk out front. But that couldn't last forever. Still Marie couldn't bring herself to ask him to resume watching Alyssa yet. Come to think of it, she didn't even know what his plans were now that his father was gone. Would he return to Deschutes Rejuvenation? She swallowed away her dread at that thought.

Alyssa stepped back and cupped both of Reece's cheeks in her little hands. "I makded you something."

"You did?" Reece's brows went up. "What is it?"

Marie's heart melted like warm caramel. The man was so good with her daughter. Had she blown their last chance with him? She swallowed.

Alyssa flipped back the cover of her drawing pad and turned over a couple of pages before she paused on an image she'd drawn.

Marie's breath caught.

It was an image that had been in the slide show. One of Reece, his dad, and his mom at one of his Little League games years ago. Marie was once again taken aback by how the picture could at once look so good and yet still be plainly evident that it came from the pencil of a child.

Reece's eyes had remained dry all day from what Marie had seen, but they misted now.

Alyssa carefully tore the page from her book and handed it to him.

Reece turned it around and simply stared at it.

"I didn't mean to make you cry. Don't you like it?"

Reece chuckled. "I like it very much, Alyssa."

"Well, why are you crying, then?"

Another chuckle escaped him, this one warm and low. "That's a good question."

"Alyssa..." Marie rested a hand of admonishment on her daughter's head at the same moment that Reece reached to ruffle her hair.

Their fingers tangled. Slowly his attention honed in on her face, his expression seeping into seriousness. Marie wanted to blurt out her feelings right then. But it wasn't the time. She would wait. She squeezed his hand and stepped back. "Come on, Alyssa. We need to go."

Reece looked like he wanted to protest, but at that moment another family approached and he was forced to stand to accept their condolences.

With a heavy heart for all he was going through, and knowing she'd been a part of it all, Marie forced herself to walk away.

Chapter 17

The days after the funeral moved slowly. She'd thought she might see him at church on Sunday or even the Wednesday night Bible study, but he didn't come to either. She was thankful Taysia was such an understanding boss, but it wasn't going to work to keep bringing Alyssa with her to the gym no matter how good she was at entertaining herself. Still, Marie couldn't bring herself to call the grieving family to see if they could continue watching her daughter, either.

The Saturday two weeks after the funeral, Dakota had planned a beach party. Alyssa was a little bit stir crazy going straight from work to the apartment and back, so Marie had agreed to attend even though it meant getting up and going somewhere when all she really wanted to do was lie around the house all day doing nothing.

She pulled her Corolla into one of the spots in the parking lot near the beach they were meeting at and helped Alyssa from her seat. "Ready to build a sand castle?"

"Yes!" Alyssa performed her signature native dance.

Marie chuckled. "Okay, let's get your stuff out of the trunk."

Despite the ever-present Pacific breeze, the sun had managed to warm the day to perfection. Lugging her and Alyssa's beach paraphernalia, Marie spotted Dakota and a group of several people from the church just down the beach a ways and headed their way. She plunked her beach chair down and wrestled it open with one hand and then rested the remainder of their items on it to keep at least some of the sand at bay.

Dan was leaning over the fire pit getting a blaze going.

Marie pressed her lips together, realizing it was nice to see him, since she hadn't seen him since he walked out of her apartment that night, but also realizing how little she'd paid attention to the fact that she hadn't seen him. Whereas, every day without Reece in their lives felt hollow and empty. "Hi, Dan." She offered him a friendly smile.

"Marie." His smile wasn't so congenial, and she hoped the pain she could see in his gaze wouldn't last too long.

"Mama, can I go play?" Alyssa hopped up and down, her pink plastic shovel in one hand and the matching bucket in the other.

Marie tweaked her little ponytail. "Sure. I'll be right here. Remember the rules."

Feet beating a hasty dash toward the water, Alyssa called, "I will! Hi, Mr. Jackson!" And then she was past him and darting toward the waterline.

Marie watched her until she fell down on her knees at the upper sweep of the waves' reach, digging like a madwoman. She smiled. Alyssa loved to dig a hole and watch it slowly fill up with water. Keeping half an eye on her daughter, she turned to Dakota. "Can I help you with anything?"

Dakota waved a hand. "No, no. We're all here to relax. Just sit down and enjoy yourself. We might do volleyball later."

Doing nothing sounded heavenly. Marie dragged her chair out to where she'd be closer to Alyssa in case she needed her and then sank into it and pulled her book from her bag. But she didn't open it yet. Instead, she tipped her face to the sun, enjoying the crisp smell of the salty air, the call of the gulls cavorting on the air currents above her, and the constant rush of the waves that never stopped beating at the shore. Alyssa chattered happily to herself something about princesses and sand castles. The sun spread warmth that the soft breeze kept to optimum.

She sighed. All this goodness, and the only thing she could think about was what she was missing. *Who* she was missing.

She glanced up the beach. The Serenity Shores property line started just a mile or so north of here. Then all she'd have to do would be to walk up the path to the house. Had she given him enough time? Two weeks wasn't very long to grieve your father. But maybe she could help him through some of it. At least be there with him through it. That is, if he took her back.

Without giving it another thought, she stood and stretched out a hand to her daughter. "Alyssa, do you want to go for a walk?"

"Sure!" The tyke leapt up, flinging sand in an arc as she spun around in excitement.

Marie laughed. "Okay, come on. Bring your bucket, and we'll collect some shells while we walk."

"Yay!"

The sand slipped and crunched beneath their feet, and Alyssa darted this way and that, running ahead to snap up a shell, running back to show it to her before dropping it triumphantly into her bucket.

Every step that took her closer to Reece prickled her skin with awareness of what she was about to do; ramped up her pulse with the fear that she was too late; dried out her mouth till she feared she'd be unable to say anything to him at all.

And then she looked up and saw the figure sauntering toward her from the direction of Serenity Shores, and all her symptoms ramped up tenfold.

Tawny loped toward them, tail wagging.

"Tawny!" Alyssa dashed ahead to meet the dog.

But Marie couldn't pull her attention from Reece.

Barefoot and wearing swim trunks and a muscle-hugging T-shirt, he looked better than any guy had a right to.

"Mr. Reece!" Alyssa abandoned Tawny, bucket, and shovel and ran full tilt toward him, arms and legs stretching as far as her little body could make them.

They were far enough away when Reece snatched her up and swung her around that the waves kept Marie from being able to hear what Reece said to Alyssa, but close enough that she felt the impact of his gaze all the way to her toes when it reconnected with hers.

Never breaking eye contact, he bent and set Alyssa down, then started slowly toward her again.

Move! She was supposed to be the one going to him. She didn't want him to ever doubt her feelings for him again. Her feet felt like they were fitted in cement, but she forced herself to take first one step and then another, and even if they did meet a bit on her side of middle, he didn't seem to notice or care.

He searched her face with such a look of hunger she lost all the moisture in her mouth again and only managed to squeak, “Hi.”

He tilted his head. “Hi.”

She missed his hat. But she could tell he’d been wearing it not long before, because the indent of the rim was still visible. “How are you? And your mom?” She reached out trembling fingers to touch his arm and felt the muscles tick once, as though her touch had surprised him.

“We’re making it. Going to be fine. Just”—he swallowed—“missing him.”

Marie nodded. Then nipped nervously at the inside of her lip. Maybe this wasn’t the right time to tell him... She glanced back down the beach toward the fire pit and the group of people who were tiny specks in the distance. “Were you coming to join us?”

He nodded. “I was. Dakota invited me.”

Dakota.

He studied her intently. “Were you coming to see me?”

Her hands trembled, but there was nothing for it but to press on, now. She certainly didn’t want to continue on not knowing what the future held. Good or bad, in a few moments she’d have his answer. “I was.”

His brows rose, and a spark glinted in his eyes in a way that made her heart leap with hope.

She spared her attention for a quick check of Alyssa. She had Tawny by her side and was digging another hole, well out of the reach of the waves. Satisfied she was safe for the moment, Marie took a step nearer to Reece. “I’d like to talk to you for a minute?”

He leaned close to her ear to whisper. “You can have more than a minute.” When he pulled back, humor sparkled in his expression.

She smiled, appreciating his attempt to put her at

ease. A driftwood log rested on the beach in an area that would allow her to keep an eye on Alyssa as well as focus on their conversation. She motioned to it. "Sit with me?"

He held his hand out in a gesture for her to lead the way.

As soon as they were seated side by side, she plunged in before she lost her nerve. "Your dad said something to me the Thursday before he passed away."

Reece fidgeted, but held his silence and only waited for her to continue, his gaze fixed along the horizon.

"He reminded me not to think of God's grace as too cheap to cover my sins." Marie picked at a splinter in a knob on the log. "You were right, Reece. And I know I might be too late, but I think we can maybe make this work. If you are still—"

He was suddenly before her, gripping her shoulders. "Are you saying what I think you're saying?"

She swallowed. "I'm saying if you'll have me, I'd like to see where this thing between us goes."

He gave such a loud whoop, she flinched, and then laughed aloud as he swung her around. When he stopped the dizzying twirl and settled her on her feet, she collapsed against him, hands resting on his shoulders.

"If I'll have you?!" He tucked her into the crook of one arm, tipping up her chin with the fingers of his free hand. "I've been missing Dad. But I've been missing you almost as much these past few weeks."

She wet her lips. "I've missed you too. I was coming to tell you...to talk to you, that Saturday."

"I wish you had. Then we could have walked through these last couple of weeks together."

She closed her eyes and relished the caress of his fingers along her jaw. "I just wasn't sure, Reece. I didn't know whether you had played that song for me to ease me into living without you forever, or if you really meant you'd be waiting."

His breath fanned her cheek as he leaned closer. "Know this, Marie Sinclair...for you, I'll always be waiting. Waiting for the next moment I get to spend with you. Waiting to hear your laugh. Waiting for the next time I can see you...touch you...kiss you."

She lifted her lips and whispered against his, "You don't have to wait for any of that, right now."

And as his lips claimed hers, Marie's heart soared. She lost track of all the sounds surrounding them except one—the sound of two hearts beating as one.

Excerpt from *Song of the Surf*,
Pacific Shores, Book 3
Coming Winter 2015

Chapter 1

Dakota Trask wanted to weep with exhaustion and Monday hadn't even closed up shop yet. The gloomy evening light reflected softly from her computer screen, doing nothing to disguise the evidence before her. She couldn't believe LoriMay had done this. Scooting her chair closer to her desk, she leaned toward the screen and clicked the button to tally the column of numbers again. She grunted when the sum came out the same as before. This couldn't be right, could it? The income showed a great deal more than the expense side, yet there were only a few cents left in the account according to the bank statement. So what had been purchased that hadn't been recorded? Her stomach rolled over on a wave of dread. Or at the very least, where had that withdrawal gone?

Dakota rubbed her temples. How was she to balance the ministry's budget when nothing seemed to be matching up?

She dropped her forehead onto her arm. "Lord, I didn't sign up for this. Everything needs to be revamped and reassessed from the ground up!" If she had her car she would go see Pastor Mark right now. But she had loaned her car to Marie—whose Corolla had died again, and with her wedding less than a week away. So Dakota was stranded, for now.

But wait...she smacked her forehead and reached for her phone. The account was cloud-based, so she'd just call him and see if he had time to take a look. She pressed on Pastor Mark's name and listened as it rang. The phone rolled over to voicemail. Disappointed, she hung up without leaving a message.

Maybe it would be better this way. She'd finish her assessment and have a better understanding of exactly what expenses the church would be facing to keep House of Hope operational, and hopefully a report on where the missing money might have gone.

Outside the wind picked up and whistled through the eaves. Which reminded her of another thing she'd noticed. The roofing on the place was badly in need of replacement. And the faucet in the first bathroom down the hall dripped constantly, while the toilet in the other one did the same. She needed to put an announcement in the bulletin at church for some volunteer handymen to come out and do the repairs for her.

Where had LoriMay appropriated the money for such things? Dakota breathed out a sigh and forced herself to sit up. Whatever category it came out of was probably severely lacking in funds, if all the others could be a measurement.

A headache pinched at the front of her skull. "I need coffee." She pushed herself up from the desk and strode to the Keurig she'd bought with her own money. One sip of the brew from House of Hope's ancient yellowed Mr. Coffee machine that had added its own unique taste to every pot, and she'd made a special trip into town to buy a Keurig. She thrust her mug under the spout and popped in a K Cup, then pressed "brew."

The pot whirred and gurgled and began to drip.

She glanced at her watch. Another hour and Reece and Marie would be by to get her. Striding to the window, Dakota planted her palms against the sill and leaned close to look out at the rain-sodden evening. Dark clouds hung ominously, and lightning forked in a jagged shard across the distance. The percussion of thunder followed bare moments later. The trees along the back of the property cowered in the face of the Oregon coast wind, bending farther than she'd ever seen them go before. She leaned low and craned her neck to see the tops of the tall evergreens. One of them was swaying like a skyscraper in an earthquake.

"Wow. Crazy."

Mr. Novak's garbage can fell on its side and tumbled across his backyard, spilling garbage everywhere. It crashed to a stop against the split rail fence that separated his property from House of Hope's. Dakota sighed. Looked like tomorrow would be a day of cleanup.

A branch from one of the trees snapped and hurtled through the air straight toward her. Dakota ducked on reflex, but the branch lifted on a last-second current of air and skittered across the roof.

Dakota wrapped her arms around herself, thankful to be inside on such a terrible night.

Behind her the Keurig gave its last gurgling hiss, and the scent of fresh hot medium roast filled her nostrils, making her mouth water, and her tension ease at just the first whiff. A splash of peppermint mocha creamer and life would be righted again, if only for a few minutes. She opened the door of the mini fridge in the far corner and squatted down to snag the tall bottle of creamer from the back.

A huge crash shuddered through the building, and glass shattered. Adrenaline cinched up every muscle in her body. A wall of air slapped into her. Her hand slipped, and her forehead cracked into the corner of the fridge. She gave herself a little shake in an attempt to dispel the throbbing.

She'd somehow ended up on the floor. Had she really felt air? Another gust blew over her. Yes. Definitely. The chill sweep of icy Pacific wind, and the sting of slashing rain.

Rain?

She turned over slowly, groaning as pain sliced across her temple.

Where the corner of her office had been only moments ago, thick gray clouds hung low. Flying debris rocketed by, and a flash of lightning lit up the silver needles of water falling from the sky.

Her eyes widened.

What in the world...?

Pushing her hands into the carpet, she stood and lifted her gaze to assess what had happened. She staggered a sideways step. And blinked to clear her vision. Surely she was just seeing things. Disbelievingly, her focus swung back to the window she'd stood at only seconds before. The glass was now a web of fissures and jagged shards with a frame of mangled metal. But through a larger intact section, she could see that one of the trees that should be standing tall in the backyard was no longer there. She pressed a hand to the ache in her head. "Oh, wow. This is so not good!"

Her focus swung back to the missing corner of the house and began to pick out more details. Evening had fallen quickly, but the growing dusk did nothing to hide the serrated wall and splintered siding, the section of roof, and the large trunk of a tree with jagged branches that angled across her desk.

If I'd still been sitting there... She swallowed.

Rainwater began to puddle and seep across the carpeted floor.

She jolted herself to action. "I have to do something!" She scooped her hand back through her hair. What? "Think!"

A tarp. She knew there was a tarp on the shelf in the garage. It wouldn't stop all the water damage, but surely it would minimize it some.

My computer!

Only one corner of her monitor could even be seen. The rest of it lay smashed under a splintered beam, and she could see sparks pinging off of something. The desk lamp?

Electricity first. Then the tarp.

She tried to run down the hall toward the breaker box, but her legs trembled to the point of near uselessness, and it didn't help that she was wearing her favorite mint suede heels. She finally reached the gray metal panel at the end of the hall and flung it open, feeling pain zing across a couple fingers. Where was the main switch? Daddy had always said in an emergency to throw the main breaker. This box didn't seem to have one. Of course it didn't. This house was as ancient as the tree that had just tried to kill it. She gritted her teeth and quickly began switching everything off.

It wasn't till she got to the fuse that turned off the hallway lights that she realized she had no flashlight. She flipped it on once more and dashed back down the hallway to her office. When she jogged inside, her feet splashed against soggy carpet.

Hurry!

She yanked open the drawer next to the coffee maker and snatched out the flashlight, then ran back to the fuse box. She finished throwing all the switches and then darted down the hall, following the beam of her flashlight toward the garage and the tarp and ladder that were kept there.

She would have to open the garage door manually. Maybe she should run out to assess the damage first so she would know what tools and items to bring with her to fix the hole. She yanked on the cord to disengage the carriage from the garage door motor and then heaved up on the heavy wooden monstrosity. It groaned and rattled as it trundled upward, and before it was even halfway open, rain slanted into the garage.

She hesitated. Might as well keep as much of the water outside as possible. Leaving the door where it was, she ducked under it.

A man loomed in front of her – a dark bulky shape against the gray of the sky.

Her heart lurched into her throat, pinching off her screech as she swung hard with the flashlight.

But the man was quick and dodged inside her intended blow. He gripped her shoulders and gave her a slight shake. "Dakota, it's okay. It's just me. Justus Teague. Reece's friend. We met several months ago. Do you remember?" He pulled her back under the overhang of the eaves.

Dakota swallowed and wished she wasn't trembling so visibly. Did she remember? How could she forget meeting a man she'd called "calendar worthy" when she thought he wasn't around, only to have him overhear it and tease her about it?

Despite the chill of the wind and the pelts of rain

that managed to find them in their meager shelter, she felt warmed by his presence. "Ju-Justus." It didn't matter that she'd been plotting all week how she would avoid him once he arrived in town for the wedding. She was just glad to see *someone*. "Can you help me? I need to—I'm not even sure what's happened—I was just running out to look. There was a crash, and rain, and sparks, and—" Words failed her, but her mind seemed to be working overtime. What was he doing here? Even if Reece and Marie had sent him, they hadn't planned to stop by for another hour.

Lightning flashed and Justus took her chin firmly in one hand and canted her head to an angle.

Dakota held her breath, chastising herself for noticing the wonderful spice-and-leather scent of his aftershave at this most inappropriate of moments.

With a concerned gaze fixed on her forehead, he slid his hand down her arm and pried the flashlight from her fingers. He lifted it and shone it just above her left eye. One of his brows quirked.

She angled her gaze upward to see what had drawn his attention. The beam of the flashlight illuminated a stream of red dripping from one of her eyebrows. She must have a little cut from where she'd hit her head on the fridge.

But she could deal with that later. They were wasting time here. She pushed his hands away from her face. "There's a hole in the ceiling. We need to get a tarp over it. But I need to go see the damage first." She made to dash past him even as sirens sounded just around the corner on Sand Dollar Lane.

He clasped her arm firmly and held her in place. "You aren't going anywhere. Let the fire crew take care of that for you. They'll have all the equipment to do what needs to be done. And they're nearly here. You need to be looked at by the medic."

Dakota shuddered. She hadn't even thought to call a fire department. On the mission field, where she'd grown up, you took care of your own emergencies when they happened. Her forehead throbbed and she touched it. "I didn't even think—how did they know?" Every thought she searched for seemed buried in mud.

Justus swept his hands in a slow stroke against her damp shoulders. "It's okay. I called them. Is there anyone else in the house?"

She shook her head. "No. I'm the only one here right now." She glanced toward the corner of the house where her office was. She couldn't quite see the extent of the damage to the front of the house in the darkness, but what she could see didn't look good. And she didn't know how she would finagle a tarp around those upthrust branches. She hadn't thought about maybe needing a saw as well.

Hopelessness begged for entrance. Her shoulders slumped. Fine, if the firemen would do that for her, that would be great. It wasn't like she was dressed for roof rescue at the moment, anyhow. Her black, ankle-length crinkled silk skirt probably wasn't the best thing to be climbing ladders in. She turned back for the garage. "Let me just grab them the tarp."

He followed her inside, but she realized he still had the flashlight when he took her arm and shone the light on a big metal toolbox. "You sit there."

"I have to—"

"Dakota, it's too late for the house. It's not too late for you. Sit."

There was an edge of something in his voice that made her follow his instructions.

"Thank you. Be right back. Don't move." He disappeared into the house.

The exasperating man had taken her light. And she hadn't even gotten the coffee she'd been looking forward to! She dropped her head onto one hand.

It only took that moment of sitting to recognize she was trembling from the top of her head to the tips of her toes. She pressed her quaking hands between her knees and winced as pain took a leisurely stroll through her wrist. She tucked her lower lip into her mouth and chose instead to cradle her arm against her chest.

She closed her eyes and saw again the tree toppled over her smashed desk. The orange sparks arcing into the darkness. The missing corner of the house.

She almost laughed as she realized that only a few minutes ago she'd been worried about a leak in the roof.

Would insurance cover something like this? Would the church hold her responsible? Was there something she could have done? Should she have insisted the trees be inspected when she took over the ministry for Marinville Assembly? She'd only been working this job on her own for two weeks. Before that she'd let LoriMay handle all that sort of thing.

Still cradling her wrist, she leaned forward and pressed her forehead into her knees.

She shuddered as she remembered Justus's question about other people. Thankfully Riley Ross was the only resident living here right now, and she'd gone with Marie to run wedding errands.

Riley. Tears threatened. Women like her were the reason it was so important to keep this place running. And as if she wasn't carrying a big enough burden trying to figure out how to keep House of Hope afloat, she had no idea how she was going to be able to help Riley.

Dakota had only been working here a few weeks, and Riley was the first woman she'd ministered to who had lost so much. And LoriMay had up and quit unexpectedly only a week after Riley moved in. That had been two weeks ago.

Dakota had no experience helping a woman who'd been beaten by her boyfriend so badly that she'd lost her pregnancy of six months. She had no experience at keeping a passive expression when looking into an eye where the sclera was totally red due to the fist that had burst the vessels there. Riley's broken arm and ribs Dakota could deal with. There were doctors and prescriptions, and heaven knew she had certainly had her fair share of nursing experience. It was the wounds left on Riley's heart she was having a hard time figuring out how to heal.

A hand touched her shoulder and jolted her back to the present. Justus squatted in front of her.

As she sat up something stung her eye and she swiped at it.

Justus moved her fingers away from the area and pressed a soft cloth to her forehead. "Hold this." He guided her hand back to press the cloth in place, then squeezed her shoulder. He set the flashlight on the floor beside her, the light spilling across the concrete floor. "Stay put for a couple more minutes while I get a paramedic to look at you, alright?" He jogged toward the half-open garage door before she could even give a response.

She nodded, but when she heard the squawk of a couple radios she realized she should probably go talk to the firemen. So, as soon as he was out of sight, she stood.

Dizziness drained through her and she bumbled a

couple of steps and threw her arms wide to catch her balance. But the floor seemed to tip up to meet her. Everything turned fuzzy and her fingers lost their grip on the cloth Justus had just given her. Her legs betrayed her and became useless limp ropes. She gave her head a little shake to fight the tug of gravity and blackness, but lost the battle and slumped to the floor.

Cold. The cement floor in the garage was very cold.

Chapter 2

Justus ducked out into the rain and jogged toward the paramedics who were just exiting their vehicle. "I've got one person injured," he yelled through the rain and wind. When the paramedic looked up, he could tell the man hadn't heard his exact words. Justus pointed to the garage and motioned for the man to follow, then turned and ran back toward Dakota.

As he loped up the drive, he tossed a glance at the huge tree thrusting across the roof from the backyard. A shudder quaked through him. He'd been driving down the street when he'd seen the tree give way before the wind. He was in town for Reece and Marie's wedding on Saturday, and they'd forgotten they had an appointment with the minister this evening, so had asked if he minded picking up Dakota.

He hadn't minded in the least, and in fact had headed this way a little early. He'd been looking forward to seeing her again. Probably more than he'd been willing to admit to himself until he'd seen that nasty cut on her forehead, and witnessed her determination to do all in her power to lessen the damage to the house. He was so glad someone had been here to stop her from climbing up onto that roof in her condition. The gash on her head was definitely going to need stitches and she might even have a bit of a concussion.

He ducked back under the garage door. Dakota lay sprawled on the floor, her face, illuminated by the weak beam of the flashlight, ghostly white. "Dakota!" Terror clawed through him, and he dashed to her side. Why had he left her alone? His hand trembled as he fumbled to find her pulse. And then she moaned and pushed herself partway up.

"Easy, Dakota. I think you passed out."

Even as he spoke she unsteadily tried to stand again.

"Whoa!" He lurched forward, gripped her shoulders, and guided her back onto the tool chest. Those crazy high heels she was in weren't doing her any favors. Squatting before her, he heard the paramedics enter behind them. "You're hurt worse than you realize. But the paramedics are here. Just let them have a look at you."

A guy with "Marinville Fire and Rescue" emblazoned on the front of his jumper, squatted before her with a med. kit. He pulled a small penlight from his pocket and peered into Dakota's face. "Hi there. My name is Luke. And this is my partner, Joel. We're just going to do a quick assessment to make sure you are safe, okay? What's your name?" The guy's light paused on the once-again bleeding wound on her forehead, and Justus tightened his fists and refused entrance to the images of another blood spattered woman that threatened to usurp his attention.

"D-Dakota."

Justus eased out a breath. At least she still remembered her own name. He started to back out of their way, but Dakota shot out one hand and clutched his arm. Her fingers slid over his forearm till they found his own. Her small hand trembled in his grasp. He swallowed and in that moment he wouldn't have moved for a million dollars. "I'm not going anywhere, just let them look at you."

The first paramedic continued to ask questions while the other shone his own light into her pupils, over her forehead, and then down to the wrist she held gingerly in her lap.

Justus heard air hiss between his teeth. Her arm was blue and swollen.

The paramedic named Luke kept speaking to Dakota in a calming tone, even while he pulled bandages and gauze from his kit and spouted some medical jargon to his partner. It was the words "overnight observation" that set Justus's heart to thumping so hard he was afraid the medics would hear it and turn to examining him next. His hand tightened of its own volition around Dakota's.

Lord, haven't I had enough of ambulances and hospitals for a lifetime?

Once again he forced the memories that tugged for his attention to the back of his mind and concentrated on the here and now.

Blood streaked one side of Dakota's hair, turning the long blonde tresses into a dark, matted clump. Even though a white bandage now compressed the wound, he could see blood already seeping through it. As the medic lifted her arm to examine it more carefully, she tucked her lower lip into her mouth and scrunched her eyes closed.

His stomach bucked. He hated that he couldn't save her from the pain.

The sound of firefighters clomping through the yard and yelling to one another rose and fell with the force of the wind.

Justus dropped his head down, staring at the blackness between his knees. The flash of another night so similar to this would no longer be abated. A night with so much more blood. So much more tragedy. So much more evil. A night filled with police and a manhunt for Treyvon McAllister, a boy-not-quite-turned-man who had so much of his life left ahead of him, but so much rage filling his heart.

He clenched his jaw and wrenched himself back to the present in time to hear...

"Would you like your boyfriend to accompany you on the ride to the hospital?"

Dakota's gaze flashed to his, her eyes widening. "No, I'm fine. I can get myself there."

The medic shifted in an uneasy way that raised Justus's concern several notches. "I'd really like to encourage you to ride in the ambulance. We'd like to stabilize your arm a little better, and keep a careful watch on your head wound there." The man tilted her a smile that tightened something inside of Justus. "Riding with us won't be so bad. Joel might even tell you a few jokes along the way." The man chuckled, and despite Justus's annoyance over the slight flirtation, he appreciated the guy's attempt to lighten the situation.

Both medics had eyed the structure overhead a few times and he knew they were considering the soundness of the building, since the other end had been smashed by the tree.

Justus didn't bother correcting their misperception over his relationship with Dakota. He wouldn't abandon her for anything, but he was going to need his wheels once he got to the hospital. "You should ride in the ambulance. I can't have you getting blood all over the inside of my Z3." He winked at her. "Will you be okay if I follow right behind you to the hospital?"

"O-of course."

The paramedics both scowled like he was the lowest form of humanity.

But it wasn't them who changed his mind. It was the disappointment he saw flash through Dakota's eyes. He tilted his head and squeezed her fingers gently. "Never mind. I'll just leave my car here and ride with you."

"No. It's alright. You don't have to." A frown pinched her brow.

"It will be fine. I'll just have Jalen drive it over for me later."

"Jalen?"

He brushed off her question. Jalen had worked with him for seven of the eight years he'd been at Deschutes Rejuvenation. And since Reece had known them both during his time working there, Jalen was also one of the groomsmen. The fact that the man was probably here more to talk him out of quitting his job than to be in the wedding didn't need to be mentioned right now. "Let's just get you to the hospital, okay?"

"Wait, what about the hole in the roof? The flooring will be ruined if we don't cover it."

Justus almost chuckled at her persistent concern over the crazy tarp. Instead, he touched her shoulder. "Let's just worry about you first. Besides, a single tarp isn't going to be able to cover that hole out there."

She swallowed. "It's just...I'm responsible."

A long damp strand of hair had fallen over her eyes, and he tucked it behind her ear, stirred by her distress. "I know. But there's nothing you can do about a tree falling on the house. Right now the best thing you can do is to get yourself better. You can deal with the damages later." He gently prodded her to her feet.

The paramedics rolled a gurney near her and helped her climb onto it. And as Justus followed her into the back of the ambulance he cast one more glance toward the house. He swallowed at the sight of the huge tree and the caved-in end of the house. Things could have been worse. So much worse.

Dakota woke to weak rays of sunshine and a dusky hospital room. Her brow furrowed. What was she doing here? She rolled her head toward the sound of a cart trundling by in the hallway, and pain sprang up from every corner of her mind. Her eyes fell shut and a low moan escaped.

A rustle of movement sounded on the other side of her bed and despite the throbbing she forced her neck to turn toward it and squinted a peek. The motion was at least tolerable this time.

Justus Teague, looking like he'd just woken up, sat on the front lip of a leather chair with wooden arms that couldn't have been comfortable to sleep in. He scrubbed fingers back through his blond curls, standing them all on end at protruding angles, and then met her gaze with a sleepy one of his own. "How are you feeling?"

Confusion plucked at her. She scrunched her eyes closed and tried to remember how she came to be here. It was only a moment before everything came back to her in a rush. She focused on Justus again, choosing to ignore his question because somehow she thought he might overreact to the fact that her head felt like it could possibly split open at any second. "Thank you for riding with me to the hospital." A flash of memory – her clutching his hand – pressed her lips closed in embarrassment. She averted her gaze.

He stood and lifted a cup with a straw to her lips. "Not a problem. I'm just glad I was there to help."

She realized how thirsty she really was, and that her voice had sounded dry and parched a moment ago. She guzzled like a dying woman at a desert water hole, then sank back against the pillows and sighed. "Thanks."

He tipped her a nod.

Pain pulsed through her skull again. "Do you think they might have some Tylenol I could take?"

Something tightened his features and he strode toward the door. "I'll get you a nurse."

He was back only moments later, a nurse bustling on his heels. "Your man here says you're hurting? Where is your pain, hon?"

Her man? Dakota didn't look toward Justus who was already back in his chair on the other side of the bed, but she would have loved to see the expression on his face over that misperception. Realizing she'd left the nurse waiting for her answer, she responded quickly, "My head."

"Well, that's to be expected considering the blow you took last night. Anywhere else?"

Dakota slowly assessed the other regions of her body and informed the nurse of a slight twinge in her left ankle and a larger one in her right arm.

"Also to be expected since your x-rays and scans revealed a fracture of your arm and a sprain to your ankle."

Dakota nearly groaned. How was she supposed to walk down the aisle for Marie's wedding in less than a week if she had a sprained ankle? She didn't even remember them doing any scans.

The nurse was still talking. "The good news is, you

don't appear to have anything more than a super mild concussion. So you'll probably get to go home here after a bit. First let's get you some breakfast and I'll put a little pain killer into your IV line." The nurse hastened back in the direction she'd come from.

Dakota didn't care about breakfast, but killing the gremlins that were kicking the inside of her skull sounded heavenly. She hoped that by "a little" the nurse meant at least a truckload of some painkiller that ended in "ine," or maybe a cocktail of several of them. Her eyes dropped closed until she remembered Justus was still here. She glanced over to find him, elbows propped against his knees and one cheek resting on clasped hands, studying her. Weariness draped his features, and the blond stubble he normally wore trimmed close and carefully groomed, looked a little thicker than normal.

"Have you been here all night?"

He nodded.

"I'm surprised they let you stay."

A grin transformed the tired lines of his face. "Let's just say it took a little bit of charm and a whole lot of persistence."

She offered him a weary smile. "Thanks for being here, but you don't have to stay. Go home and get some rest."

Humor tucked around the edges of his eyes. "I can't have all these nice hospital staff thinking I'm the worst boyfriend in the world."

She laughed, then, as shards of fire shot through her head, gasped and stiffened.

Justus was standing by her side in an instant. "Sorry. What can I do?"

She eased out a breath and wrinkled her nose at him. "Don't make me laugh. At least not till a few minutes after she gets back with that painkiller."

He touched her shoulder, his face serious. "You got it."

His total seriousness almost made her laugh again. She opened her mouth to tease him about it, but just then Marie and Reece knocked at the open door. She changed her intended words. "Hi, you two. Come in."

They stepped into the room, followed by Riley and a dark haired Hispanic looking man she'd never seen before.

Marie rushed to her side. "Dakota! I can't believe it! I hardly slept last night, I was so worried about you. Are you going to be okay?" She leaned over the bed and gave Dakota a gentle hug.

Dakota patted her back. "I'm going to be fine. Where's my munchkin?"

"Darlene is watching her this morning."

Reece's mom seemed to have come around one hundred percent in her opinion of Marie over the last few months. Dakota was glad about that. Especially for Marie's four-year-old daughter Alyssa's sake.

She moved on to a more pressing matter. "I just hope this isn't going to ruin the wedding."

Marie waved away her concern and rejoined Reece at the foot of the bed. "Our wedding should be the least of your worries. I can't believe a tree fell on House of Hope!"

"Crazy, huh?" Dakota tried not to wince when Marie rested one hand on her sprained ankle at the end of the bed.

Reece pushed his ever present cowboy hat back on his head and folded his arms. "So what do you hear about when you get to make your escape?"

Dakota offered a thin smile, feeling her energy

already beginning to flag. "The jailer said I'm up for parole this morning sometime."

Just then the nurse stepped back in carrying a breakfast tray. "Well, look at you, Miss Center of the Party." She offered Dakota a wink as she set the tray on the rolling bedside table. She pulled a syringe from her coat pocket and reached for Dakota's IV port. "A few painkillers and you'll be up and dancing with one of these handsome guys in no time."

Everyone chuckled and Dakota couldn't remember being happier to see a syringe full of drugs in her life.

A warm hand settled against her shoulder. "You alright?"

She forced herself to meet Justus's concerned scrutiny. "I'm fine."

He stepped over to his chair and pulled his black leather jacket from the back. "Tell you what. We'll all let you eat and we'll run grab a bite ourselves. Then I'll be here again about ten to see if you've been released and to give you a ride, alright?"

As nice as it would be to simply agree and let him control the situation, he'd already done more than enough. Besides, she knew from talking to Reece that Justus had done time. How safe could it be to be alone with him, no matter how secure he made her feel?

She arched her brows at Marie. "Actually, if Marie's done with my car I can just drive myself?"

Marie darted Reece a look, then Justus. Neither man seemed to want to meet Dakota's gaze. But there was compassion in Marie's eyes when she looked at her. "Um... We sort of don't want you driving yourself anywhere, at least for a couple days.

Dakota's brows shot up. "We?"

Marie winced and swung a finger to Reece, then on

to Justus, and back to herself with a tiny nod.

"Guys! I'm a big girl who bumped her head. I'm perfectly capable of taking care of myself and don't need you babying me."

Justus cleared his throat. "You have a slight concussion. A broken arm. And a sprained ankle. Be reasonable." Without giving her another chance to protest he turned to the nurse. "So will ten be a good time to check back?"

The nurse agreed that the timing should be about right and adjusted Dakota's table. "You just eat when you are ready, okay?" With that she made her way from the room.

Despite her grumpiness over their three-way conspiracy, Dakota liked the feeling of being taken care of – especially by Justus – just a little too much. How was it she could so enjoy the company of an ex-con? Her parents were always thousands of miles away on another continent, and she'd simply adjusted to doing for herself, she supposed. But now...she met Justus's warm blue eyes filled with concern and her heart sped up in a way it hadn't since Jason. *Jason.* There were so many reasons why she needed to avoid a relationship right now – especially with a guy like Justus – and she suddenly felt a little desperate to avoid the impending alone-time with him.

She tore her gaze from his and settled it on Marie. "Marie, Justus has already done more than enough. Couldn't you pick me up then?"

Marie shook her head. "Sorry, Reece and I have to run to Portland today to grab the supplies for the reception. But Justus has already offered to be your chauffeur for the next couple of days. And Riley's going to drive your car out to Serenity Shores for you so it will be there when you are able to drive yourself again."

The next couple of days? Her pulse picked up at just the thought, and she hoped no one was studying the display on the monitor next to her bed too closely.

Do not make the same mistake twice!

Her gaze flicked to Justus once more. What had sent him to jail?

Jail time wasn't the only drawback to the man. She distinctly remembered his death-trap of a red motorbike. She lifted one brow at Justus, unable to hide her pique. "You going to make me ride behind you on your motorbike?" Her chest tightened at just the thought. She'd sooner walk home than straddle a bike ever again.

But he only shook his head. "Left my bike back home this time. Brought my car, instead." He tipped his head at the Hispanic man. "Jalen there protested over having to ride with the wind in his face the whole way here. Good thing too, I guess."

Jalen, standing quietly, arms folded, smirked and shook his head over the obvious misrepresentation, but tilted her a nod of greeting.

She wiggled her fingers in return, since moving her head still hurt like crazy. "So Riley, you aren't going to Portland with Marie and Reece today?"

Riley shook her head.

Dakota studied the woman. Her face was as impassive and unreadable as usual. Dakota sighed. At least she didn't have to worry about Riley's safety from her ex-boyfriend since he'd driven his car off the coastal highway and been killed instantly the night he'd last beaten her up. Even so, Dakota didn't want Riley to be alone. She had so many emotions roiling through her right now.

Dakota pressed her lips together, not wanting to make her feel self-conscious in front of all those in the room, but not wanting to leave her to be on her own all day either.

Jalen saved her from the dilemma. "If Riley doesn't mind, Marie asked me to deejay for the wedding reception on Saturday, and I could use some help checking out the church's equipment and doing some sound tests."

Dakota liked the man already. She looked at Riley and waited for her reply.

Riley shrugged and gave a tiny nod.

And Dakota offered Jalen a smile of thanks.

He lifted his chin in a quick nod to indicate it was no big deal, shoved his hands deep into his pockets, and scuffed one toe at the floor.

Marie broke the awkward silence that settled. "Thanks for letting me use your car yesterday. That was a big help.

"You're welcome. But I'm not happy that you guys are all ganging up on me." Dakota stuck her tongue out at Marie.

Marie only chuckled. "I'm sure you'll get over it." But her gaze traveled to Riley, who stood quietly, her focus sweeping each aspect of the room as if to memorize the space.

Dakota was suddenly hit with a concerning thought. "Riley, where did you sleep last night? Are you okay?"

Riley's attention zoomed to her, then flicked to Marie, but she didn't speak, only nodded and tucked a strand of her straight red-blonde hair behind one ear.

Jalen looked down and kicked at something on a tile near his feet, his jaw jutting off to one side.

Marie hastened to speak for her. "Riley stayed with

Alyssa and me last night, and she's welcome to stay until we get another place figured out...."

Marie's words trailed away, and Dakota knew the implication. She was welcome to stay until something else was figured out or until Marie's lease ran out at the end of the week when she and her daughter would move into Serenity Shores with Reece.

Which brought to mind another thought for Dakota. *She* didn't have a place to stay either. Where was she going to go when she left here today? The fire department had condemned House of Hope, and all of Dakota's and Riley's belongings were in there.

Reece seemed to be able to read her thoughts. "Listen, with the wedding coming up, we didn't book any guests at Serenity Shores for about three weeks. We'll have plenty of room for you two plus all the wedding guests. So no need to worry about where you're going to stay."

Relief rushed through Dakota. But it was Riley who concerned her. She offered the woman a smile. "Sounds good to me. What about you?"

Riley shrugged and nodded, still offering no word or flicker of emotion.

Lord, help me to reach her. "Good. It's settled then. Thank you, Reece. That lifts a big weight from my mind."

Everyone started to head for the door then, but Dakota needed to know the truth about Justus before any more time passed. "Reece? Could I talk to you for a minute?" Thankfully everyone seemed to get the hint that she wanted a word alone with him, and Reece lingered while everyone else left the room.

She picked at the blanket, trying to determine the best way to ask her question but no diplomatic turn of phrase came to mind. Finally she just plunged in. “Listen, I know he’s your friend...but didn’t you tell me Justus served time? Should I be careful about being alone with him?”

Reece actually chuckled. “No. Not at all. There’s no one you should trust more than Justus. He did serve time, but that’s his story to tell, and I’m sure he’ll get around to telling you someday. But you don’t need to question your safety with him, and trust me when I say he’s a different man now, and there’s no need for concern.”

Dakota chewed the inside of her lip. No need for concern except she might lose her heart to the guy! “Okay. If you’re sure. Thanks. Sorry. I—” She waved a hand, unsure what else she wanted to say.

“I’m totally sure. Don’t worry about it. You’re in good hands with him, I promise you. You good now?”

“Yes. Thanks.”

He nodded and stepped out into the hall.

Dakota released a soft sigh as she lifted the lid from her plate of food. All she really wanted to do was sleep, but she’d force a few bites down first.

And try not to think about the enigma that composed Justus Teague. How did an ex-con engender such loyalty from his friends? When it came down to tallying pros and cons for potential men to date, “previous prisoner” was definitely a big mark in the “con” column. Not to mention his obvious thrill seeking, daredevil, need-for-speed side. But in the “pro” column she’d have to mark down a man who’d slept the whole night in an uncomfortable chair for a woman he barely knew just so she’d have someone close by in case she needed anything. And those blue eyes that probed every nuance of her face with a soft compassion that drew her like a warm fire on a cold day. Definitely those.

She gave up trying to understand the complex swirl of emotions spinning through her, pushed the food tray away, and sank against the softness of the pillows.

Unfortunately, exhausted as she was, sleep remained elusive. First the doctor came in on his morning rounds. He double checked all her injuries, assessed the response of her pupils to light, listened to her heartbeat, and checked her blood pressure and pulse. He offered her a gentle smile. "You are lucky, young lady. Your injuries could have been much worse."

Dakota swallowed. "Yeah, I think God was watching out for me. I was sitting at my desk right where the tree fell only moments before it happened."

The doctor gave a little whistle. "Well, however you were spared, you've managed to escape with only a slight concussion, a few stitches, and injuries that will heal within a few weeks." He jotted something in her chart. "I'll write up the order for your discharge and you are free to leave as soon as the nurse brings by your prescription for pain killers. The stitches on your forehead will dissolve on their own, and I'll take a look at them at our appointment next week." He glanced at her chart again. "I see you've had malaria. Had any flare-ups recently?"

"No." She shook her head.

"Good. Well..." He stood. "We'll get you out of here as soon as we can."

Dakota figured she'd better hear the bad news straight from the horse's mouth if it was going to be bad news, so she took a breath and asked, "I'm in a wedding on Saturday. Will I be able to walk by then?"

To her surprise the doctor nodded. "Your sprain isn't too severe. I'd like you to wear this ankle boot until

Friday, but I think it will be okay to remove it and participate in the wedding on Saturday. Just listen to your body. Too much pain means it's not ready yet. Any other questions?"

Relieved at the answer, Dakota shook her head.

"Alright then..." The doctor stood and shook her hand. "Sometimes a trauma like this, especially one that results in exhaustion, can cause a relapse of the malaria. So please take it easy over the next few days for sure and give yourself lots of rest."

She smiled. "The way I feel now, my body will be demanding that from me."

"Good. Listen to it!"

Dakota had just once more settled into her pillow to hopefully find a few moments of the doctor's last prescription, when a knock at the open door revealed Pastor Mark poking his head inside.

"Hi Pastor." She waved him in. "Thanks for coming by."

Pastor shook his head as he approached. "I'm so glad you are okay!"

Dakota made a face of regret. "I'm really sorry about House of Hope. Is it going to be fixable?"

Pastor Mark held out a hand to reassure her. "Don't you worry about a thing. The house is insured, and just a year ago the insurance company had a man come out and check over those trees at our request and expense. He gave them the all-clear to remain. So I have every confidence that the damage to the house will be fully covered. The most important thing is that you're okay."

Relief washed through Dakota so palpably she realized how much her concern had been weighing on her. "I'm so glad to hear that."

He folded his arms. "Of course House of Hope has

been condemned until repairs can be made. Police Chief Tom Hansen said to just give them a call when you want to get some of your things and he'd have an officer meet you on the scene. Riley said anytime would work for her."

"Okay, thanks for letting me know."

Pastor looked chagrinned then. "I saw I missed a call from you last night." He winced. "I really hope you weren't trying to get a hold of me after the tree fell?"

She rushed to reassure him. "Oh no! That was before. I wanted to talk to you about the books. There are some things not seeming to add up in the accounting for House of Hope."

"Oh? What?"

"Well, to me it looks like some money may be missing somewhere."

Pastor Mark's eyebrows peaked. "That doesn't sound good."

"Is there a time I could come by and we could look at the numbers together? You might know something I don't with regards to it."

"Sure." Pastor pulled out his phone and consulted his calendar. "How about next week some time? After you have the wedding out of the way? Say Tuesday afternoon about two thirty In the meantime I'll take a look at the account myself to see if I can find the discrepancy."

Dakota smiled, relieved to know she could talk to him about it. "That sounds good."

Pastor stayed and prayed with her and visited until Justus stepped back into the room. Pastor Mark stood from where he'd seated himself in the room's chair.

Freshly showered and groomed, the sight of Justus, and the sweep of his swimming-pool-blue eyes, stole all the moisture from Dakota's mouth. "Pastor Mark." The words rasped and she cleared her throat and started again. "Pastor Mark, this is Justus Teague. He's a good friend of Reece's and here for the wedding. Justus, this is our pastor, Mark Rolland."

Justus nodded and stepped forward to shake the man's hand.

"Well." Pastor Mark turned back to her after greeting Justus. "I'd better be going. Mrs. Murton is in here too. Got struck by a branch when she was out walking her Pomeranian last night."

A surge of sorrow and guilt shot through Dakota at the mention of old Mrs. Murton. But Pastor Mark wouldn't know that a good deal of the woman's loneliness was Dakota's fault. Mrs. Murton wouldn't know either, for that matter. Dakota forced her lips to form words. "Oh, I'm so sorry to hear that. Is she going to be alright?"

Pastor nodded. "Yes, she just cut her arm pretty good, and they wanted to keep an eye on her blood pressure overnight. But her call this morning said it was stabilizing. Anyhow, just say a prayer for her, if you would."

"I will. And I'll stop by to say hello to her on my way out. What room is she in?"

"Just down the hall in room 307. Thanks for praying. I know she'll do the same for you." He lifted a hand of farewell, then paused. "I'm assuming you have all the help you need, and a place to stay?"

Dakota nodded. "Yes. Thank you."

"Good. Well, you just let us know if you need anything, alright? And I'll be seeing you soon."

After she signed discharge papers and received her prescription, Dakota fought her casted arm and booted foot to dress in the same clothes she'd worn the day before, while Justus waited in the hallway. The sleeve of her blouse wouldn't fit over the cast and she had to tear it to get it on, and the Velcro on the boot snagged her skirt several times before she managed to smooth it into place. Finally she sank down onto her bed to slip on one shoe. Why, oh why had she chosen yesterday to wear the mint shoes, she wondered as she thrust her good foot into one of the high heels and tossed the other shoe into the small bag the hospital had given her.

Task number one accomplished, she eyed the crutches leaning next to her with some trepidation. Task number two was to get herself to Justus's car without making too much of a fool of herself.

But how was she to use the crutches when one of her arms was casted and hurt every time she moved it? "Lots of weight on the armpit and you'll just have to use your hand to swing the crutch forward. Come on. You can do this."

Her little pep talk didn't make her feel much better, but she forced herself into motion and stood. She balanced precariously on her heel and tucked the crutches under her arms, then fumbled to loop the canvas bag's handles over her head.

Thankfully, the door to her room was a sliding one that was easy to open.

Justus waited for her, one shoulder planted into the hallway wall and arms folded. His black leather jacket stretched tight over his broad shoulders and looked way too good. It made her self-conscious of her messy hospital hair, lack of a shower, and probably barely-there-smudges of makeup.

He stood when he saw her. "Ready?" His gaze swept down and paused on her shoe before rebounding to her eyes. His lips twitched. "I better find you a wheelchair."

"No. No. I'll be fine. I have to get the hang of this sometime. Might as well start now."

She awkwardly swept the crutches forward and did her best to ignore the throbbing in her arm. The hospital bag swung out and then flopped back against her belly like lead weight on a plumb line.

Justus stepped up right in front of her and relieved her of the bag. He didn't move back but stayed where he was, looking down into her face. "What's your middle name?"

Her brow puckered. "Jean. Why?"

"Jean's so normal. I figured it might be stubborn or obstinate or something like that." He winked.

She swung her good hand to smack him, but he just laughed and ducked away. "Come on gimpy. The elevator's at the end of the hall. We'd better get started if we want to make it home by tonight."

"I just want to swing by Mrs. Murton's room on the way out."

But there was no need to search out her room, because a grey haired woman in a hospital gown was coming toward them from the other end of the hallway. She smiled and waved.

Dakota's heart filled with love and dread all at once – just like it did each time she saw the woman. "Hi Mrs. Murton."

"Dakota, dear! It's so nice to see you! Well, not here necessarily, but you know what I mean." She smiled.

"It's good to see you too. Are you going to be okay?"

Mrs. Murton waved away her concern. "Pastor Mark told me about the house. I couldn't believe it." She reached out and squeezed Dakota's good hand where it rested on the padding of the crutch's handle.

"Yes. Pretty crazy. But the worst that happened is my

broken arm."

"Bones do heal, I suppose. I'm very glad you weren't hurt worse." The truth of her words shone in the older woman's expression.

And threatened to bring Dakota to tears. "Thank you." How she wished the past could be different.

Mrs. Murton's soft blue eyes angled toward Justus, and a glimmer of curiosity and interest registered. "Who's this nice looking man, dear?" The tone of her voice said the elderly widow would be the highest bidder if Justus were on an auction block.

"Uh..." Dakota looked down and scrubbed at a mark on the floor with the tip of one crutch. That nurse must have given her a dose of some crazy drug, because she was suddenly experiencing a hot flash she felt sure could be seen on satellite from space. "This is Justus Teague. He's in town to be in Reece and Marie's wedding on Saturday."

"Oh, he knows the Cahill boy?" Mrs. Murton assessed him from the top of his blond head to his black leather work boots and back. "Well, he must be alright then." She offered Justus a smile that he returned with an offered hand.

"Nice to meet you. Mrs. Murton, is it?"

"Yes, dear." She accepted his handshake into a two handed grip and leaned close to speak right into his face. "You take care of my Dakota, you hear? No hanky panky. She's a good girl."

Justus blinked. "Yes, ma'am." He glanced over and grinned at her.

Somewhere in a scientific lab, there were meltdown-danger sirens sounding a warning because of the heat flash surging through her. Dakota wished for a fan. Or maybe just a straight-up ice bath. Her cheeks felt like they might be on fire.

And Mrs. Murton only made it worse by turning to her and pinching her chin. "I'm glad you have found someone else. Jason would be happy for you. Well…" She stepped to one side and continued down the corridor, waving to them over her shoulder. "If I ever want them to let me out of here I have to prove that I'm capable of walking this hallway without my blood pressure going through the roof. So goodbye for now. I'll see you at the wedding, I presume."

"Bye." Dakota willed away the guilt the mention of Jason brought and glanced at Justus, half expecting to be grilled about who he was.

But all he said was, "She seems like a lady who cares for you very much."

Dakota forced herself to head for the stairs. "Yes. She does."

Despite her insistence that she would be just fine walking to the car, Dakota had never felt more thankful than when she sank into the warm leather seat of Justus's BMW Z3. Her leg trembled from exhaustion, and her arm was hurting like nobody's business.

She relaxed into the seat and scanned the interior as she waited for him to stow her crutches in the trunk and get in on his side. Burl wood accents glowed golden against the backdrop of the black leather interior. The heated seat button beckoned, and she clicked it to the "high" position, already feeling a bit of a chill after leaving the warm blankets of her hospital bed. Hopefully it wouldn't take too long to heat up after he turned on the car.

She scanned the sky outside, amazed at the beautiful day. No one experiencing today would ever think that just a few hours ago the wind had been howling so ferociously that it had knocked a tree over on her house. Cloudless blue skies. Slight breezes. Sunshine. Weak December sunshine, but sunshine nevertheless. It was like a new blank page. A new opportunity. Maybe something better would come from all of this? She sighed.

Okay, Lord. We'll rebuild. One day at a time. One life at a time. Give me the strength I'm going to need to get the job done.

Justus sank into the driver's seat and glanced over at her. Once again she was taken aback by the azure blue of his eyes. She tipped her head against the headrest and worked her teeth over her lower lip. *Cons, Dakota, cons! He's an adrenaline junky who spent time in jail for who knows what. And just look at this car. It might have four wheels, but if ever a car revealed something about the personality of its driver, this is it.* No. He was definitely not the type of man she wanted to get into a relationship with again, no matter how much her fingers itched to reach out and touch the prickly, thick five o'clock shadow on his cheeks.

His gaze roamed her features, lingering on the spot where she knew a line of black stitches etched the skin near her temple. "You don't look like you got much rest this morning."

She wrinkled her nose and made a face, taking a fortifying breath at the reminder of just how terrible she must look. "Nor a shower. Nor clean clothes. I'm a mess. Do you think we could stop by the house on our way out to Serenity Shores Bed and Breakfast and grab some of my things? I just have to call, and they'll have an officer meet us there. Riley said anytime was fine with her."

He looked dubious. "Why don't you let me run you out to Reece's place and then I can come back in and grab some stuff for you?"

The thought of having Justus fetching her clean underwear burned embarrassment across the back of her neck. "Um, I'd rather just stop there myself, if you don't mind. It's on the way and will only take a few minutes."

He sighed. "Like I said...stubborn runs thick in your veins."

She couldn't help a giggle. "My daddy used to say they put my picture in the dictionary next to 'pigheaded.'" The fingernails of her good hand bit into her palm. What had made her simper like a teenager in love for the first time? It must be the exhaustion making her giddy.

Humor softened the concern tightening his features. "I'll have to remember that." He sat back and inserted the key. "Make the call."

She eased out a breath of satisfaction. "Thank you."

He grinned. "I bet you didn't often have to fight very hard to get your way either, did you?"

She pursed her lips and thought back to her childhood on the mission field in Africa. "Guess not too often. Why?"

He laughed outright then. "Because any man looking into your big blue eyes would sooner melt into a puddle than deny you a thing."

Alarm shot through her. However she forced a smile and when he looked over and offered a crooked grin, batted her eyelashes with great fanfare.

But as he pulled out of the hospital parking lot she turned her focus to the scenery out her passenger window and buttoned down all the heartache that had just threatened to explode all over everything. No way could Justus know the memories those few words had jostled loose. Neither could he know it had been her begging and pleading that had led Jason straight to his own death.

And almost to hers.

Chapter 3

Justus berated himself as he pulled the car to a stop in front of House of Hope. He didn't know what he'd said, but he'd obviously said something wrong, because the normally talkative Dakota hadn't said a word since they left the hospital parking lot.

Now she clipped out, "The officer should be here any minute."

He glanced over at her, but she hadn't budged, so he peered out the windows toward the house, not wanting to push her by asking what the matter was.

Caution tape cordoned off most of the yard. And it looked like a crew had been by to remove the tree, based on the lack of protruding branches and the huge swath of plastic sheeting tied over the gaping hole in the roof.

She clicked her fingernails against the cast on her right arm, tapping out a rhythm reminiscent of the "William Tell Overture."

Finally he reached over and stilled her nervousness.

Her gaze leapt to his.

He tried not to notice how good her slender fingers felt beneath his own, because a relationship with a woman, no matter how beautiful and enticing she might be, was the last thing he needed in his life right now with the mess it was in – even if he hadn't been able to think of much for the past two weeks other than how he was looking forward to seeing her. "I'm sorry."

A furrow ticked her brow. "For what?"

He released her hand and eased back to his own side of the vehicle. "I'm not sure. I think I said something that upset you."

She shook her head. "It wasn't you...." Her words trailed off, and her focus blurred against the dashboard for so long he was just about to reach over and still her fingers once again when she seemed to shake off her melancholy. "Well, we aren't going to get my stuff just sitting out here, are we?" She reached for her door handle.

Justus touched her shoulder. "Let me get your crutches. Sit tight." He wanted to pry for more details, wanted to know what thoughts churned the cogs behind those beautiful blue eyes of hers. But he let her have her space and climbed from the car.

Bringing the crutches to her door, he waited till she'd swung her legs out and then reached in to grasp her good arm and pull her to her one good leg. When she was standing at full height her head came to just under his chin, despite her crazy shoes. She clutched his arm in a fireman hold to catch her balance and looked up. And he felt the power of her azure scrutiny all the way to his toes. For a moment he forgot the crutches clutched in his free hand. Her forearm was warm and smooth beneath his hand, and before he realized what he was doing he'd stroked his thumb several times across the inner pulse point at her elbow.

Dakota swallowed visibly. "Justus—" She broke off whatever she'd been about to say and tore her gaze from his, then reached for the crutches. "Why were you here last night? I hadn't even heard you were back in town, yet."

He gave himself a mental shake and stepped back, but not so far that he wouldn't be near enough to catch her if she lost her balance. "I came a few days early, and Reece and Marie had an appointment with the pastor, so they asked me to come get you at six."

She angled him a look. "You were there just after five."

He shrugged and considered his response. He might as well test the waters a little. Forbidden though they might be. "Maybe I was looking forward to seeing you."

"Right!"

"What? You don't believe me?"

She tilted her head. Narrowed her humor-filled eyes. "You could have gotten my number from Reece at any time and gotten in touch over the past several months. But you didn't. And I'm supposed to believe you came by early because you wanted to see me?"

That was true enough. Did he dare admit to her the number of times he'd almost asked Reece for her contact information? He folded his arms and leaned into his heels. "Maybe I'm shy."

She laughed and shook her head. "No."

He couldn't resist the smile that begged for release. "Maybe I was worried you wouldn't take my call or respond to a text."

"You should have been worried about that. Because I for sure would have ignored you, just so you know." There was a hint of sass in the look she gave him. But as she tried to swing a step forward her ankle boot caught against the crutch, and with her other foot in the totally impractical high heeled shoe she started to topple.

He lunged forward and grabbed her waist, getting his shin clipped by a crutch for his trouble. He forced his lips to stretch into what he hoped she would mistake for a grin and looked down at her, arching one brow.

Her eyes were a bit wide, but other than that, she seemed fine. “Thanks.” She wrinkled her nose sheepishly.

He gave her a little space and moved the conversation back on track. “Maybe my life has been so complicated lately that there hasn’t been room in it for a relationship.” He nearly winced. He hadn’t meant to strike so close to the truth.

She frowned and seemed to ponder his words as she adjusted the crutches.

He waited till she had them settled firmly under her arms. “You good?”

She leaned into them and nodded.

He gave her a little more space, still keeping a close eye on her in case she needed help again.

“Complicated I can understand. Which brings me to what I wanted to say…”

He waited quietly, not quite sure what to feel. It might be a relief if she told him she wasn’t interested. Would certainly make things easier and less complicated.

“I wanted to say thanks again for staying with me last night. I wasn’t really feeling like myself, and I hope I didn’t make you feel obligated in any way.”

He stepped out of her path and folded his arms. He tightened his jaw, a little bit terrified over just how much it had meant to have her to reach out for him last night. He spent so much of his life being rejected by the boys he was trying to help; being let down – even horrified – by their actions. To have someone actually reach to him. Need him. Want him nearby. Well that feeling was quite unlike any other. But he couldn’t tell her all of that, because that would just sound loony. So what he said was, "I stayed because I wanted to."

"Well... thank you. It's just...I remember grabbing your hand and..." Her cheeks turned a pretty shade that brought to mind strawberries and cream on a warm summer day. She crutched a couple steps and glanced down the street, muttering something to herself that he didn't quite catch.

But it reminded him of the first time he'd met her. The time she'd been talking to herself and he'd overheard her call him "calendar worthy." He grinned at that. And just then she turned and caught his humor.

Her cheeks brightened another shade. "I'm talking to myself again, huh?"

He gave in to the urge to tease her a little. "It's okay. I've learned some enlightening things while listening to you talk to yourself."

She laughed uneasily. "Justus, I know I said..."

Her expression begged for his help, but he was having too much fun with this to let her off easy. "You said what?"

She squinched her nose at him. "You know exactly what I said, but I want you to know, that just because I said you were...nice looking, doesn't mean I can be in a relationship right now." The sincere set of her gaze said she hoped her gentle rejection would be taken seriously.

He eased out a breath. The words had hurt a lot more than he'd expected them to. But this was good. And what else was he to expect? He felt pretty sure Reece had told her about his time behind bars. A couple times he'd seen a hint of curiosity mixed with fear on her face as she studied him. He gave himself a mental shake. Yes, this was better. "I'm actually glad you said that, because while I also find you attractive, I wasn't really kidding about what I said. My life is in a bit of chaos right now and it's not really a good time for me to be in a relationship."

Dakota eased out a silent breath. See? She'd known he was only being a nice guy who didn't want to hurt her feelings. And what she'd said was mostly true. She really *couldn't* be in a relationship right now. But it wouldn't have hurt her feelings much if he'd at least pretended like he'd wanted a bit more than friendship from her. At least he'd said she was attractive. She'd have to live with that, she supposed.

His brows arched as he waited for her reply.

She pursed her lips and forced herself to nod like all was as she'd hoped. "Good. So...friends?" She leaned in to her crutches and held out her casted hand to him.

He stepped close and gently gripped the fingers protruding from the end of the plaster. "Friends." His touch was more like a soft caress, as though he feared he might hurt her if he squeezed her fingers too hard.

A zing of awareness zipped up her arm and down her spine. Oh boy. Maybe the handshake had been a mistake. She tugged to be released, but instead of letting her go he moved into her personal space, maintaining his gentle grasp. And when her gaze flew to his, he grinned. "I'm going to like being your friend, Dakota Trask."

And I'm going to be tortured to only *be yours, Justus Teague.*

He swept a glance toward her shoes. "As your friend can I just say for the duration of the time you are on crutches, it would probably be best to wear flat, practical shoes?" He winked.

She stretched out her leg and angled her mint suede

spool heel back and forth. "What? You don't think these are the best crutching gear?"

The squad car pulled up just then and Tom Hansen stepped from the vehicle.

Justus moved back and Dakota smiled at the Police Chief. "Hi, Chief. Couldn't find anyone else to babysit me, huh?"

He chuckled. "Unfortunately, there was a lot of damage last night and all my officers are occupied elsewhere." He swung a look to Justus.

Dakota pointed the end of her crutch at him. "This is Justus Teague. Justus," she swung a gesture back toward the officer, "Chief of Police Tom Hansen."

Justus nodded and shook the man's hand.

The chief ambled up the walkway to the front door. "Riley coming?"

"She should be here any minute. I called her when we were leaving the hospital. Thanks for letting us in to get our stuff."

Tom smiled at her over his shoulder. "Sure. We can't have you ladies living without your shoe collections."

Justus's laughter floated on the wind. "That would be a tragedy for sure!"

Dakota chuckled and felt heat sear her cheeks. "It is true. I can't wait to put on my Vans!"

www.ingramcontent.com/pod-product-compliance
Lightning Source LLC
LaVergne TN
LVHW091043080826
845145LV00002B/608

* 9 7 8 1 9 4 2 9 8 2 5 5 5 *